The Beast Beneath

The Beast Beneath

A Novel by Mark Wyckoff

ISBN 978-1-105-42537-0

SYNOPSIS: In this new age haunted house story, based on actual events, Tyrone, a successful black physical trainer, his long-time love and her three children find themselves on the verge of losing both their minds and their souls. "The Beast Beneath" is set in the mysterious, historical area known as New Monterey, where Tyrone and his family have just moved into an old house on Newton Street.

At first, the place seems like it may bring the family together, but Tyrone soon discovers that the house has other plans. Under its malign influence, Ty soon finds himself and his family acting strangely. He begins to hear a horrible series of sounds emerging from beneath the old house and begins to investigate-with harrowing results. As he researches the house's background, Ty comes across a newspaper story from the early 20s that may hold the secret to the danger posed by the old, weather beaten residence. His belief is cemented by an encounter with what he believes to be the ghost of a young boy who perished tragically there nearly a century ago.

As Ty's conviction grows, however, his girlfriend Jackie refuses to believe his tales, blaming the sights and sounds instead on his drug use. Ty, however, through a series of increasingly terrifying experiences, becomes utterly convinced that their new home is, in fact, an ancient house for specters, devils and demons of all description.

The family is increasingly fractured by Ty's obsession and Jackie's denial. Some of the three children have also seen the house's spectral residents, increasing the tension. But when Tyrone comes to believe that their young daughter Caroline is being singled out for attack by the ghost of the young boy, he acts, contacting a legendary healer from the East Coast, who teams up with a priest in order to conduct a cross-country battle to put a century old soul to rest.

As the story continues, a surreal battle is waged in which Tyrone becomes convinced that he must maintain the belief that his family is truly in peril in order to protect them. To this end, he attempts to sober up, hoping to prove to both Jackie and himself that his perceptions are not the product of the pipe, but of some obscene rift between normal existence and another, darker world of flame, fury and depravity.

Ty's attempts to clean up, however, are constantly endangered by drug-using friends, Jackie's own fondness for cocaine and the distress created by the nerve shredding experience of living in a house under constant attack by its supernatural residents.

The story is told almost exclusively from Tyrone's viewpoint, allowing the reader to decide whether the spooked-out events Ty reports as taking place in the house on Newton Street are indeed real, or the product of a fractured mind. As the story progresses, the evidence that evil truly does exist in the house becomes more difficult to ignore as even Jackie and the youngsters begin to encounter the apparent legions of the unliving who have settled in a private hell located beneath this old house.

An internal battle is soon being waged within Tyrone as well. He is virtually pulled apart by the spirits beneath the house and falls back into drug use, urged on by Jackie who is herself beginning to psychologically disintegrate under the pressure being exerted by the house and its darker denizens.

Finally, the family does what any sensible group of people would do in such a situation-they prepare to get out of the old house as quickly as possible in order to move on to a new life.

But departure is easier said than done as the spirits use every weapon at their disposal to destroy the family and drag them down beneath the house on Newton Street where they would join the loathsome rave being staged by its unholy inhabitants.

The family's escape from New Monterey proves a nerve-jangling adventure, with the spirits pursuing Tyrone and his teenage son Ben until they are forced to spend an entire night on the most dangerous street in town. It is there that Tyrone must find the redemption he desperately needs, the separation from New Monterey and its temptations he must attain before the family can truly move on. While they wait out Ty's dark night of the soul, he and Ben are visited by ghosts of a different kind-lost souls, hopeless drunks and drug addicts and even one women who begs to come along. By the time the sun rises, they will have gotten a true glimpse into hell on Earth.

"The Beast Beneath" is much more than just a hip-hop haunted house yarn. Tyrone's battle for his soul-and the souls of his family-is presented with a shocking realism not seen in traditional ghost stories. In order to save himself and his loved ones, Tyrone must become more than a movie-style action hero. He must find the strength and faith within himself to recognize, battle and, ultimately, escape an evil force ravenous for new souls to fill its empire beneath the battered old house on Newton St.

BOY HURT IN BLAST . . SHOOTS SELF DEAD

Joseph Hillzer, 8, suicide after painful injury.

June 25, 1923, 8 year old found, dynamite cap near
his house left by a grading crew. It exploded leaving
him badly wounded. He ran home with his sister
trying to stop his bleeding but couldn't face
disfigurement for the rest of his life and worried that
it would break his mother's heart. So he ran into the
house and got a .32 caliber revolver from his
mother's dresser and shot himself through the
heart. He was a precocious child having passed the
eighth grade examination.

Mark Wyckoff: Biography

Mark Wyckoff was born April 17, 1958 in Orleans, France. At the age of two, he and his parents arrived in California, where Mark attended Monterey High School as a football stand-out. He graduated in the year of America's Bi-Centennial, 1976 and pursued a life-long interest in physical fitness. He spent three years in the Army and 28 years in civil service.

Mark participated in competitive bodybuilding and continues to work primarily in the field of physical training. "The Beast Beneath", based entirely on actual events, is his first novel.

His goals include writing, travel and, in particular, educating youth on the perils of drugs and the importance of self-discipline, clean living and creating a new generation of leaders. "I hope this book will find its way into the hearts and minds of those readers who need it most desperately," says Wyckoff. "And that's a demographic that includes the majority of human beings walking the planet. There's a Beast Beneath each and every one of us, just waiting for a moment of weakness."

Chapter 1

Tyrone had always been a very capable person; analytical and in control whenever possible. Everything had to be just so, to the point where he was often teased about his perfectionism. But all that seemed to change when he moved with his girlfriend, Jackie, her two boys, Jason, 17, Ben, 14, and their daughter Caroline, seven, to an old one-bedroom, one-bathroom house in Monterey, California in February 1997.

Jackie also had a daughter from a previous marriage—Carla, who was one year older than Jason, Carla and her boyfriend, John, moved into an apartment together across town following their high school graduation.

Jackie meanwhile had rented an old house on Newton Street from a friend. Tyrone knew nothing about this since Jackie never spoke of it, but he really didn't have much say in the matter since she had only rented the Newton place for herself and her two boys. Tyrone agreed with Jackie, that he and Caroline should live together, since her hands were full with Jason and Ben. Tyrone and Caroline only planned to stay at this house on Newton Street for a short period anyway, until he could find a more permanent place for them.

Tyrone had been dropping broad hints at Jackie regarding his desire that she move away from California. Unfortunately, he knew that she would not be able to make such a move any time soon as Jason was turning 18 and wanted to stay in California after he graduated. Nonetheless, Tyrone decided to leave California sometime in February 1998, hoping it would give Jackie enough time to prepare for the change. He didn't want to leave Jackie behind because it would mean taking Caroline away from her. But a fresh start away from California and the sordid life they were living is what was really needed.

Jackie and Tyrone grew up in a little town called Seaside where everyone knew everybody. Jackie called Tyrone "Ty." He liked that. Seaside sat right off the ocean, where the beaches were always filled with the sights and sounds of family fun. There were mountains for hiking, lakes for boating, and beautiful scenery to enjoy.

Jackie was raised in a strict military environment. Everyone in her family was also musically inclined. At the age of ten, Tyrone developed a schoolboy crush on Jackie who was a year older than he. She and two friends had formed a singing group that was rocking the town at the time. The group would travel from school to school, winning every contest they entered. By the time Jackie got to high school, she was not only a local celebrity; she was touring as a background vocalist for Sammy Davis, Jr.

When Jackie returned from her tour, Tyrone introduced her to Larry. Tyrone's family and Larry's had lived on the same street, and over time they grew up together. Then Larry's family moved to New York and he and Ty lost contact. When Tyrone learned that Larry and his family were back in town, he couldn't wait to tell his old friend about this beautiful singer and cheerleader he was in love with. Tyrone also told him that he hoped to one day marry her.

With Larry having been away for a while, Tyrone didn't notice the change in him at first. But it didn't take long to realize that the "new" Larry was only out for himself. Worse, the girls in school wanted to know all about the new guy.

Tyrone felt there was no way that Jackie would be interested in Larry. He was only a sophomore and Jackie was a senior. Tyrone completely missed it, but Jackie and Larry became lovers soon after he introduced them. For the rest of Jackie's senior year, Tyrone tried to make it as difficult as possible for her. Hurt and miserable, Tyrone went to football games and yelled profanities at Jackie while she tried to concentrate on cheering for the team. He sat in the stands and made a jealous fool out of himself.

Only later did Tyrone admit how much he loved her.

Along with the entire school Tyrone could only look on as sophomore Larry walked around campus with Jackie, the girl Tyrone wanted to marry. Meanwhile, Larry would lie to Jackie and cheat on her with her best friends. It was hard for Tyrone to watch someone so sweet and gifted being treated so badly. Finally, 1975 ended, Jackie graduated from high school and registered into the local college.

Larry and Tyrone didn't see much of each other after Tyrone's family moved out of the city that summer. Their new house sat on the banks of the Carmel Valley River, which ran right through the back yard. This scenario was enhanced by a great mountain view. Tyrone did not have time to explore much beyond the ranch style home as there was too much work to be finished before sunset each day, though the property did have a wealth of interesting wildlife passing through it.

Despite the move, Tyrone continued to have feelings for Jackie. One day, he decided to get in touch with Larry and find out how he and Jackie were doing. Larry told Tyrone that they were both working; that wasn't unexpected news, given that they had both worked full time for years. Tyrone was totally surprised, however, to hear they were planning to visit Tyrone at his family's new house the following weekend. Tyrone was pleasantly shocked that Jackie would consider coming by after the way he'd treated her when she and Larry became lovers.

That Saturday Tyrone watched Larry's car pull into the driveway, the sight of Larry and Jackie together generating mixed emotions in him. Tyrone felt some uneasiness, but could hardly wait for the electric garage door to open. Surprisingly, only Larry got out of the car. Tyrone hugged Larry and spoke to Jackie as she remained seated in the car. Larry just smiled and laughed, and Tyrone saw right away that he was still the same boastful fool he'd been since boyhood. The look on Jackie's face on the other hand made it obvious that she was neither happy nor that innocent virgin girl Tyrone remembered from high school. They only stayed around for a few minutes, but as they drove away, Tyrone wished he could read minds.

The next time Tyrone saw Larry was at practice, at the start of the following football season; Tyrone made Varsity and Larry played for the Junior Varsity squad. That was pretty much it between the two of them, though Tyrone did say good-bye to Larry right before leaving for the Army. In and around school, meanwhile, Tyrone did the normal things teens do always wanting to be the best at whatever he did, obtaining a high school diploma while remaining a standout in sports. Ignoring a football scholarship, Tyrone joined the Army to escape the hard discipline at home. At least he thought it was hard at home until reality struck.

The Army was difficult. The oppression was too much. Tyrone served in Korea for fourteen months where the living conditions were poor. Nevertheless, he persevered, serving in five different stations spanning the world as a computer operator.

Completing his tour with honors, maximizing all physical training scores, and becoming an expert rifleman, Tyrone received an honorable discharge in 1979.

When he got out of the Army, he received a serious blow. Tyrone's oldest sister, Susan, who was very special to Tyrone, had committed suicide. Tyrone had stayed with Susan and her husband frequently during Tyrone's teen years and she kept in close contact with him all the while he was away in the army. Their mother, Willie Gail, died when Tyrone was eight years old. After Willie Gail's passed, it was very hard being brought up in a family of three sisters and two brothers while their father worked day and night to try and make ends meet.

It wasn't long after Tyrone mom died that he got a step-mom who was only thirteen years older than he. She was a very brave young white woman to take on a step-mother's role in a black family, especially in the late 1960s.

Chapter 2

Tyrone was ambitious, but he knew it was going to be hard getting over Susan's death. He took on two jobs to keep busy, keeping in contact with the family and occasionally running into someone he knew from school. During one of these meetings he learned that Larry and Jackie had gotten married in July of 1977 and Larry had enlisted into the Army not long after he did. Tyrone also learned that Larry and Jackie spent their first tour of duty in Alaska, and were now stationed here at Fort Ord, CA. One day Tyrone called Larry's parents' house, got their son's home phone number and called him.

The phone rang several times before Jackie answered.

"Hello," she said.

"It's Tyrone."

"Ty!" She sounded surprised and happy to hear from him. It had been three years since the two last spoke.

"Ty, where are you?"

"Here in Monterey," he said.

"What are you doing now? Are you still in the Army?"

"No, washing dishes from 8 A.M. to 4 P.M. at the Tuck Box in Carmel and stocking shelves at the Fort Ord commissary from 5 P.M. to 3 A.M.," he answered.

"Well that doesn't leave time for much; do you have a girlfriend?" she asked.

"No one special at the moment. How is Larry doing?" Ty quickly changed the subject.

"He's ok and if you're not working tomorrow—are you?"

"It just so happens I'm taking tomorrow off," Ty answered.

"Well then come for dinner and you can surprise Larry and meet my little family."

Ty accepted the dinner offer and gave Jackie a number so he could be reached if there were any changes. Ty and Jackie exchanged a little more small talk and Ty got directions to get to Larry and Jackie's house before hanging up the phone.

That next evening, Jackie and Ty started up a friendship that would last over the next six years. Tyrone tried to stay neutral regarding Jackie and Larry's rapidly declining marriage. Larry's lying and deceptions were finally catching up with him.

Tyrone bought his first house with his two brothers and a sister-in-law at the age of twenty-one. Tyrone had grown up a lot since joining the Army. He really wasn't wild about the idea, but his family was all for it, so he gave it a try. Unfortunately, the situation deteriorated within six months and he moved out.

Tyrone then turned his attention back to a daily regimen of working out and physical training. He had worked out extensively in the past, and had been staging weight lifting exhibitions at his parents' house since the age of twelve. At the age of thirteen, Tyrone conducted his first fitness consultation. While in the Army, Tyrone continued to perfect his skills. Before long he joined the National Physique Committee and became a head judge for the Armed Forces bodybuilding competitions. Tyrone competed and did very well, which led to his playing the role of Hercules in a regional production of "Heaven Sent." Tyrone then opened his own personalized training facility and became one of the founders of a health products line. He married and divorced twice during this period, the first marriage lasting thirty days, and the second surviving five years.

In the meantime, Larry managed to throw away both a career in the military and his marriage to Jackie after landing in jail on drug charges. It was during that six year period that Jackie and Ty decided they both wanted to expand the nature of their friendship. They also expected it would be a shock to everyone once their feelings become known. However, they had no hint of the roller coaster ride upon which they were about to embark.

During Jackie's final break-up with Larry she moved from houses to condos, and then to apartments, trying to match a budget with a baby and two very young kids. Tyrone tried to focus on his own career but worried constantly about Jackie's situation.

As time passed, Larry's unwanted attempts to reconcile with Jackie failed, just as Jackie and Ty failed in their attempts at living together with Jackie's three kids. It got to a point to where Ty not only wanted, but he felt he needed a child of his own. Jackie agreed and gave birth to Caroline.

Five more years went by, and Larry had now moved to a city two hundred miles away. Soon thereafter, Jason moved in with his dad. Tyrone had had to chastise Jason several times for disobeying Jackie and felt it would have eventually come to blows had Jason stayed. Ben, on the other hand, was quiet and easy-going and did whatever he was asked to do. By the time Carla got out of high school and moved out of the house, Jackie, Ben, and Caroline and Ty were ready to make another go at living together as a family.

This arrangement lasted only two-and-a-half years; then, unexpectedly, Jason returned from the city in need of a place to stay. That was when Jackie decided to rent the old house on Newton Street for herself and the boys, and Tyrone decided to sell his house.

Chapter 3

Jackie drove Tyrone over to the old house on Newton Street in Monterey to show him where she was going to live, so he could start moving some of her things there. The place was old with a mysterious quality. It was very small and constructed entirely out of wood. It was painted a pale yellow with white trim and sat high off the ground with open beams running underneath the structure. As Jackie and Tyrone circled the place, peeking in the windows, Tyrone couldn't help disguise the look of distaste that showed on his face. The house was really run down and needed painting inside and out.

"Why are you looking that way?" Jackie asked.

"Why do you think?" Ty replied. "This house is a mess, just look at the trees and plants there; it looks like a damned jungle!"

The tone of Ty's voice kept Jackie quiet for a minute as he continued his dissection of the house, moving as he spoke. He stopped suddenly in a corner that gave him the sensation of being in an ancient, forgotten graveyard.

"When was the last time someone lived in this tragedy of a house, Jackie?" he barked.

She answered quietly, "I don't know."

It sat on a very large lot. There was a shed behind the house. It also had a strikingly tall two-story barn, as old as the house. Without another word, Ty took the key to the house out of Jackie's hand and headed back toward the front door without taking an eye off of the tall barn that gave Ty such an uneasy feeling.

"So what does the landlord keep in that barn?" he asked, exasperated, not bothering to wait for an answer. Jackie stood there puzzled, staring up at the window on the side of the barn. The sound of the front door opening got Jackie's attention, and she almost ran Ty over as she rushed to get into the house.

"Hey! What's the big idea scaring me like that?" Ty demanded. "I could have had a damn heart attack, Jackie!" A pause, then Ty added a sarcastic note: "Did you see anything up there in that barn window?"

"Hell no, Ty! The landlord is using that barn to store a lot of old family things; that's why there's a lock on it. And if you think this damn place is so bad you can stay as far away as you like," she added.

Jackie started getting loud and mad.

"Just bring all of my damn things here; that is all I want you to do," she insisted.

"Calm down Jackie, I was just teasing," Ty said, his blood pressure dropping as he continued to walk toward the tiny bathroom.

In that bathroom sat the oldest tub he'd ever seen. It stood on legs, and had massive lions' paws.

"Jackie, come take a look at this bathtub," he said.

"Wow! Now that's different!" she replied. Neither Jackie nor Ty was angry any longer.

She gave a faint smile, and then they hugged and kissed their way into the bedroom. They stood holding each other swaying back and forth, the floor creaking loudly. Ty looked down at the noisy floors. Jackie followed Ty's eyes. He then shot Jackie a look and she loosened the grip she had on Ty and said, "Quit acting so stupid!"

Jackie then stalked out of the room and into the kitchen, the floors creaking as she passed. The old floor was nice, but a complete refinishing and polishing, along with filling the holes, would make it look brand new.

In the kitchen, off to the right, was a small laundry room that had a back door secured by a lock in need of repair. The kitchen cabinets needed refinishing and more shelves. In short, a complete remodeling would do the trick. But the old house on Newton Street had potential after all, and Ty promised Jackie he would work on it.

They both got their last looks, pointing out various objects of interest to one another. An old chandelier that they had somehow overlooked earlier hung down from the ceiling. There was also a built-in chest beneath a couple of windows in the dinning area. Ty opened the chest and was surprised at its depth. It's a good place to put clothes, he thought. He also liked the sun room; it had a very large window, he told Jackie.

Speaking of windows, the house was absolutely festooned with them, with more windows than one would think necessary in a house twice its size. Ty tried to open one, but it appeared to be sealed; perhaps from the last paint job the house received. There was no telling how long ago that had been.

As Jackie got into the car, Ty locked the front door after one last glance.

He got into the car and started it. "Well this is it," he said.

"What did you expect? You know what we're paying. Can't beat the price."

Realizing that she didn't have a choice, Ty tried easing Jackie's thoughts and reassured her that everything would be fine as they drove away from the tiny, old house on Newton Street.

It was about a twenty minute ride to Ty's house, and they were both thinking about the work that remained to be done in the next two weeks. Finally, they arrived back at Ty's place.

"I'm going to make a few phone calls," Ty explained. "Got to make arrangements for the help and tools we'll need over the next two weeks to remodel that old Newton place."

Jackie gave Ty a hug before getting out of the car and heading inside to check on Ben and Caroline. Often, Jason would take off and go to Carla's apartment to keep away from Tyrone during the moving process. Jason knew Tyrone was not too thrilled about his return, and Jason knew that Tyrone placed some, if not all of the blame on him as the reason for their enforced move.

Tyrone got in contact with a friend named James, who owned a construction company. Ty wondered if James would be available to stop by the old house on Newton Street any time during the next two weeks to give Tyrone a hand on some of the remodeling. James told Tyrone that he was in luck; James had nothing going on, and set up a meeting with Ty to go over the details of the job.

The next morning James and Tyrone met and went to work on securing the back door and a couple of windows in the kitchen, so when it was time to bring things to the Newton house it would be safe to leave them there. They were especially concerned about the tools, which they would otherwise have to haul to and from the Newton house daily. They walked all around the old Newton place, inside and out, and made a list of everything that had to be done, as well as the materials needed to complete the job.

The excitement of a new project energized Tyrone. It made him happy to know that they would be creating a clean, new atmosphere for Jackie, the two boys, Caroline and, for the time being, himself. As the remodeling got under way, James started the repairs on the door and floors while Tyrone prepped the inside of the house for painting. During the first week, it was pretty much the same thing; lots of prepping, cleaning, and discovering still more of the little things that had to be repaired. Tyrone really didn't want to invest too much money into this old house, but some things just had to be done. Some nights during that first week he would stay later than James, trying to get as much of the painting done as he could. The excitement of the accomplishments however, often led to excesses.

Tyrone experienced premonitions, and these uneasy feelings about the old house grew as Tyrone's evening's work at the Newton place continued later into each night. Tyrone's wits were being tested by the uncanny occurrences beginning to take place there. He never divulged the episodes of fear he felt or the strange unexplainable things that had taken place at the old Newton house to James or Jackie—footsteps not his own heard in the house and the pounding sounds underneath the floorboards.

On the sixth night of that first week Jackie decided to visit James and Ty at the Newton Street house to check out the progress of the remodeling. Ty heard the car pull up, looked out the window and saw that she had brought a six pack of beer and some snacks in a bag.

"Break time," Ty yelled.

Jackie walked in the house smiling.

"Hi," she greeted Ty, and then turned to scan the scene. "Wow! This place is looking good already. It's so bright and smells so fresh in here," she complimented.

Jackie gave Ty a kiss, then turned and spoke to James as he was reaching for a beer. "Hi, James. Thanks so much for the help."

Jackie took another satisfied look around at all the work that had been done on the house while James and Ty enjoyed the beer and snacks. It was getting late, so James finished putting up the shelves in the kitchen and bathroom, having already patched the numerous holes in the floors throughout the house. Jackie and Ty thanked him again as he left while Jackie stayed behind to keep Ty company.

The first week was coming to a close, and Tyrone's house had already sold with the new owners scheduled to take possession in one week. There was still a lot of packing and cleaning at Ty's house to be done. Tyrone knew he had to push himself into the wee hours of the morning to get the inside of that old Newton house habitable as soon as possible, so Jackie, Caroline, the boys and he would have a place to stay. Jackie didn't mind staying behind to help out as it was the weekend, and she had put Caroline to bed before leaving. She had even given Ben the number where she could be reached if Caroline woke up looking for mom and dad.

As Jackie and Ty continued to work into the early morning, finishing up the painting, Ty got the feeling that there might be something other than him and Jackie in this Newton house. He kept those thoughts to himself while he worked, not wanting Jackie to see any change in his behavior.

As they were cleaning up and getting ready to leave, Jackie asked whether Ty was all right.

"I'm just tired, that's all," Ty replied.

They hurriedly finished cleaning. Ty turned off all the lights in the old house as they left and locked the door. Jackie walked down the steps, but Ty took one step and froze because suddenly he could no longer see Jackie standing only five feet in front of him. It was that dark outside. Suddenly, the keys in his hand started rattling, He turned quickly and reached for the door knob, put the key in the lock, threw open the front door in a hurry and switched on the porch light. When he turned back toward Jackie, there she was, still standing there, laughing.

"Come on, chicken," she called out.

Ty let out a sigh of relief. "My nerves are bad enough already," he confessed, "and I don't plan on falling out here in this pitch black night on top of some garbage that I do not want to be bonding with. So 'Ha! Ha!' your damn self."

They ran to the car and got in. Jackie continued to laugh throughout the drive back to Ty's house.

When they arrived, they were both dirty and tired. Jackie got cleaned up, while Ty fed Cass and locked up everything before getting into bed. Jackie let Ty sleep into early Saturday afternoon while she got up and made breakfast for Caroline. When Ty did wake up, he lay in bed for a while just thinking about that old house on

Newton Street. He couldn't help but wonder if he had really sensed something unnatural living there. One thing Tyrone did decide—he was going to work at his own house this coming Saturday and Sunday. He only had the floors to finish at the old Newton house; the outside could be cleaned up once Jackie got all moved in.

Tyrone was rolling out of bed as Jackie came into the room to see if he had gotten enough rest and offered to fix something to eat while he got cleaned up.

"A couple of sandwiches and a glass of juice will do, thank you." Ty answered quietly. There was a lot of packing to be done and it wasn't the time to try and talk to anyone about what he thought he had experienced at the old Newton place. It could have been anything—or nothing at all. A long hot shower was just what he needed to get his thoughts back on track.

Afterwards, Ty came into the kitchen, gave Caroline a big hug and thanked Jackie again for the help the night before. Ty told Jackie what the plans were for the weekend. He could see that she was very tired.

He told Jackie to lie down and catch up on some rest and not to worry, he would cook dinner tonight. She agreed and slept for the rest of the day. He didn't bother asking where Jason and Ben were; eventually he would need their help, but the less he mentioned Jason's name in any conversation with Jackie, the better they got along.

Tyrone started packing and stacking boxes in the garage. Ty's things were going to be stored out of state; he had already made plans. Ty estimated he would order a twenty-seven foot truck by the following Thursday. That's what it was going to take to haul everything away, and it would be a lot cheaper in the long run. Plus, he was hoping it would put an exclamation mark on the future move out of California.

Ben and Jason came home and Tyrone let them know when he'd need their help. He also told them to keep the noise down because their mom was asleep.

After dinner, Jackie commented on the amount of packing Ty had done while she was asleep.

"Well Ty, I must say, I'm surprised at all the work you've gotten done."

"Well, you must've been pretty tired to have slept with all the noise I was making," Ty marveled.

"You're not planning to pack any more tonight, are you?" Jackie asked.

"No! I decided I'm calling it a night."

Caroline did not like that decision; she wanted to continue packing because her room was set to go next and she didn't like the fact that it was almost bedtime.

Ben made it back to the bedroom where Jason already had changed clothes and was getting ready to leave the house.

"Where are you going?" Ben asked Jason.

"Out," Jason replied, heading for the front door.

Jackie stopped Jason and repeated the question. "Where are you going? You are not eighteen damn years old yet and you don't live in the damn city with your father anymore. You had better try asking if you can go anywhere," she stated firmly.

Ty decided to butt in. "Jason knows when he's going to be needed around here and he's only going back to Carla's house right, Jason?"

"How is he planning on getting there?" Jackie wondered aloud.

Jason answered softly, "Carla and John are on the way over in their car."

Tyrone was glad Jason was leaving and hoped the boy would wait outside for Carla and John so he wouldn't have to deal with John. Tyrone didn't care for John at all, thinking of him as a trouble maker.

When Carla and John did show up, they didn't stay long or have much to say to Tyrone. Ty didn't care, muttering a few words as he slammed the door.

"Ty!" Jackie called out upon hearing the door slam. "That was uncalled for."

"Okay," Ty agreed. "Can we just forget about it then and put Caroline to bed so we can enjoy the rest of the evening?"

Jackie nodded in agreement and they made their way to the bedroom with a bottle of wine.

The next morning arrived pretty fast, but everyone seemed to be well rested. Jackie made a nice breakfast and afterwards Tyrone got right to work on Caroline's room. Caroline was happy to be Tyrone's little helper. By lunchtime Ben, Caroline and Tyrone were all ready for a break. After lunch, Ben and Tyrone got the rest of the little things packed and all that was left were larger items. Those things would go out when the truck arrived on the following Thursday. All of Jackie's furniture was in storage close by the old Newton house, and Tyrone had made plans to move it with Larry's truck after the floors there were finished.

Jackie prepared dinner a little earlier that night and the family ate without Jason. He didn't come home or call. It was hard to say what Jason was going to do from day to day and if Jackie knew, she wasn't saying.

Sunday night after dinner Tyrone spent a little time with Ben and Caroline. It was hard for Ty to stay focused on what the kids were talking about with so much on his mind, but he managed to keep up with the conversation. Tyrone had to get to the rental shop early Monday morning to rent a buffer to finish the floors at the Newton house, although he was not looking forward to going back to that place alone.

He got up from the couch and walked into the kitchen to help Jackie with the dishes. Jackie had already asked Ty a couple of times during dinner whether everything was all right.

"You were awfully quiet tonight, Ty. Are you sure you don't want to talk about whatever it is that's on your mind?"

Tyrone just kept right on putting plates and glasses in the dishwasher in a silent daze. The things that occupied Ty's mind were subjects he didn't want to share with anyone for the time being. Tyrone's own thoughts were less certain, so he assured Jackie that he was fine and she shouldn't worry, as he reached for the trash and the dog food.

Ty went into the back yard to feed Cass and sat with her for a while.

Jackie came out for just a minute and gave Tyrone a kiss before heading back inside to prepare for bed and make sure the kids were doing the same.

A half hour later, Tyrone got up from the chair, put the trash out in the can and returned inside. The light in the bedroom was already off. He quietly made sure all the doors and windows were locked, and then climbed into bed while trying not to disturb Jackie. Tyrone lay very still, staring at the ceiling and thinking of past.

For the previous two-and-a-half years, he had been pulled apart by diametrically opposed influences in the life he lived: crack cocaine and the life-long faith and belief in maintaining a sound mind, and body. These influences cannot peacefully coexist within a person, and no matter what Tyrone tried, he was never at peace.

Tyrone thought back to 1985 and his last bodybuilding show. That night, after the competition, he was congratulated by a number of people. As Tyrone shook hands and got plenty of hugs, he noticed Casey, his oldest brother, standing by Tyrone's other brother Kenneth and their father. Casey appeared as if something was wrong. He seemed many miles away.

Tyrone walked over to them and exchanged handshakes and hugs. When Casey and Tyrone embraced, Tyrone got an uneasy feeling.

"Are you all right?"

"Yes," Casey answered weakly.

Tyrone told Casey that whatever was bothering him, they would talk about it later. They embraced one more time. Everyone was still standing around exchanging their opinions about the outcome of the show and trying to decide where to go eat. Casey and their Dad came together but couldn't stay for the celebration. They both had to work the next day.

They said good-bye to everyone and started walking toward their car.

Tyrone yelled out to Casey, "Call me tomorrow!"

Casey turned and looked back at Tyrone as he continued to walk toward their car. Tyrone's thoughts were on Casey as he returned to the post-show excitement.

Kenneth came up behind Tyrone, put an arm around his shoulder and told Tyrone to lighten up.

"You did well and it was a good show tonight. Let's catch up with Matt and Tim," he suggested. Matt and Tim Williams were brothers, two power lifters—the heavy and super heavyweight champions.

Tim and Matt rode in the front of Matt's car, and Kenneth and Ty sat together in the back. Matt started driving toward Club Rio where he and his brother hung out whenever they were in town. As soon as the car started rolling down the road, Kenneth, Matt and Tim started getting a little crazy. Tyrone's mind was still on Casey but he did his best to play along. They traveled down a back road for about twenty minutes when suddenly an animal ran out in front of the car. It was too late to stop and Matt ran over it. He wanted to go back and see what it was that he ran over.

That was when Ty yelled, "No! Keep going, Casey is going to kill his wife and himself!"

"What the hell are you saying?" Kenneth asked.

With both hands over his face Ty yelled out again "Casey is going to kill his wife and himself!"

Everyone in the car got quiet. They all just stared out the window at the big bright full moon. It was strange and cold the rest of the way to Club Rio and not another word was spoken about what Ty had said in the car that night.

That night passed, and they all made it back home. The next evening, the news reported a murder-suicide.

Casey had killed his wife and himself.

Ty was awakened by the Monday morning rush with everyone going in different directions.

"Hey there," a voice called out to 'Ty softly. "You had better get a move on if you plan on getting those floors done at the old Newton house today."

Ty rolled over, in bed looked up, and there stood Jackie ready for work. He reached over pulled her onto the bed, and gave her a hug.

"Are the kids ready for school?" Ty asked.

"Yes," Caroline answered as she raced into the room to ask her mom if they could go now.

"Ok, little school girl. Give daddy a kiss good-bye and he'll see you later."

Jackie, Caroline and Ben left and the house was suddenly quiet.

Tyrone got himself ready, eating whatever was left over from breakfast. He grabbed the list from the counter and headed out the door. However, before he drove off, he made sure there was plenty of water in Cass's bowl and something for her to eat.

Tyrone drove over to the rental shop, and when he got inside he held a conversation with almost anyone who would listen. Tyrone was stalling. There was a lot on his mind, and he knew he would have to go through some serious changes once he began living in that old house on Newton Street.

Once he had wasted enough time at the rental shop and could not let another minute go by. He loaded the equipment into the car and headed for the old Newton place. There was very little traffic on the way, which was a good thing as he hadn't paid much attention to the other drivers on the road. He was too busy going over the game plan on how to deal with those floors and the strange unwelcome feelings that he experienced each time he returned to that Newton house.

By the time he finally arrived, he had calmed a bit and was ready to deal with the bad feelings he had developed toward the strange, old place.

Tyrone got out of the car and unloaded everything onto the porch, but before he went into the house he took one more walk around the yard. On the way back to the front door, he stopped and peered at the crawl space that ran underneath the house. There was no door on it. He tried not to imagine what in the hell, could possibly be going in and out of that dark confined space.

Ty got the key out of his pants pocket and walked up the steps, taking all the time in the world to open the door.

He slowly started bringing the equipment inside. Once that was done, he went into the bathroom, then the bedroom, and from there moved onto the kitchen, checking to see if everything was the same as he'd left it.

Once he made the rounds and had seen that there were no changes in the house, he plugged in the radio, began singing and started in on the floors. Tyrone worked quickly and kept focused on working. He was determined not to be distracted by anything. He wanted to have the floors sanded and the first coat of clear put down before nightfall, so he would only have to come back once more by himself to put the finishing coat on the floors. With darkness setting in quickly, he tried very hard not to take a break. But he hadn't rested once all day and was definitely beginning to tire, so he finally decided to stop for a soda and a rest.

Tyrone sat down on a section of the floor he had not yet finished. Leaning up against the wall, he closed both eyes for just a few moments. He re-opened them just as a cold sensation began forming around in the room. He froze briefly then leaped up off the floor, looking around to see if a window or door was open to let in this cold draft. He then stood very still while trying to figure out what could have possibly caused it to become so cold in the house so quickly. All of as sudden, a thump resonated from underneath the house, drowning out the loud music he was playing.

Tyrone was badly shaken; the living shit had been scared out of him. He jumped along the edge of the floor toward the front window area he had not yet finished, to determine whether he could see anything.

But, darkness had already set in.

Tyrone hurriedly turned down the music so he could hear better. He waited for the sound to repeat but heard nothing. It became very strange and still in the house. He did not like the turn of events. He felt it was time to go.

Ty grabbed the mop and started slinging the rest of the clear solution over the unfinished areas on the floor while pulling the bucket toward the front door. Whatever was missed he did not care. He finished, put the mop in the bucket and left, closing the front door behind.

Once Tyrone was out of the house he started thinking about the open crawl space that lead underneath the house.

How in the hell was he going to get to the car, he wondered, without walking right past it?

Even though the car sat directly in front of the house, it seemed as if it was a mile away. One thing he was sure of, he wasn't going to stand on the porch and wait for whatever he heard under the house to come outside and shake hands. So he gathered himself and made a dash for the car. Getting into the vehicle was no problem, though he ripped his shirt sleeve while trying to simultaneously start the car and free himself from the damn door handle.

Tyrone was in such a hurry that he started driving down the street without even turning on the car's headlights. He didn't get very far down that dark road before realizing it—as well as the fact that he hadn't taken the time to look inside the car before getting in. Suddenly Tyrone began feeling that same cold air that had touched him back in that old house and it was coming from directly behind him.

He wanted to slam on the brakes and stop. But instead he just stared into the rear view mirror, waiting for someone or something to rise up from the floor behind the back seat. Tyrone's eyes were practically bulging out of his head and Tyrone's heart raced out of control. He quickly turned on the car's dome light and punched the headlights. He sped on as fast as he could just to get to a main street where there were more people, cars and lights. Indeed, reaching the intersection did help calm the wild sensations he was experiencing. Meanwhile, he continued to hurry toward home and it didn't take long at the speed he was going.

For a long time he could only sit in the car parked in the driveway. A knock on the car window startled him to the point to where he almost busted out the car window.

"Ty, get out of the car! What in the hell is wrong with you?" asked Jackie in a concerned voice.

He got out of the car trying not to shake quite so much. He just played it off, laughing. "Sorry honey! I'm just tired and I guess I didn't see you come out of the house."

"Wow, you must be really tired," she said, giving Ty a big hug. "You were sitting there a long time. Let's get inside. It's cold out here."

Jackie went into the kitchen to warm up Ty's dinner while he washed up and checked in on Caroline, who told Ty all about the day she'd had in school and handed Ty a book she wanted read before lights out.

"All right, sweethearts, let's get this book read before you become daddy's main course for dinner tonight," he warned. "Because daddy is starving."

Caroline laughed and held her farther closely as he read the book, her eye lids drooping as he finished.

Tyrone gave Caroline a kiss goodnight, and turned out the lights before heading into the kitchen to eat. He really was hungry, consuming two complete plates and having seconds on dessert.

Tyrone was quick to take out the trash, feed Cass, and return inside. He had plans to keep Jackie's mind off asking too many questions about the day he'd spent at the old house on Newton Street. Ty quickly told Jackie that everything was coming along great as he pulled her towards the bedroom, making Jackie laugh.

Once they finally settled down, still holding each other, Ty spoke quietly.

"Jackie, that old house has got some ways about it and they are definitely strange."

"Oh honey, it's just a house, don't look so hard into it," she said. "Sure there's history that goes along with its age," she added.

"I'm sure you're right." Ty replied, not wanting to argue the issue. He was feeling too good kissing away on Jackie's neck to be thinking any more about that weird old place, so they just enjoyed each another late into the night.

The next morning Ty got up to find everyone bursting with energy. He helped prepare the lunches for school and they sat down to breakfast together. When it came time for the kids to leave for school and Jackie to head to work, Ty passed out kisses and hugs as everyone left. He then closed the door and headed straight to the back yard and called for Cass, who came running.

"Cass, you are coming with Daddy today so eat up."

Tyrone got all geared up to apply the final coat on the floors at the old Newton house. Jackie's things were about to be brought out of storage and would have to be moved into the Newton house.

Tyrone cleaned up the kitchen, closed up everything and loaded Cass in the car, then drove quickly down the road. With Cass along for the ride he felt a lot safer. He hoped to get the floors done early so they might be dry by the afternoon and he could start that evening with everyone's help transporting the furniture. Then he could focus on getting the big truck the next day. It would be Thursday just as he had planned it.

Driving up in front of the house on Newton Street was the same experience as always. Once again he wondered what took place here and who in the hell lived here in the past. Today he did not have time to ponder these questions; he was a man on a mission. Tyrone opened the car door and Cass jumped right out over Tyrone and started sniffing around. Tyrone watched for a while and then called for her.

"It's time to get started, Cass."

Ty put Cass on a leash and they entered the house. Ty led Cass toward each room cautiously, as she pulled hard on the leash. It was difficult for Tyrone to hold onto the leash because of the perspiration in the palms of his hands. Cass's head would work left to right very suddenly, sniffing at air, keeping Tyrone on the jumping edge. Tyrone felt and sensed all that Cass did. At any second Tyrone was ready to flee the old house, but as Cass led the way throughout the house pulling Tyrone along, he saw that everything was exactly as he had left it the night before when he had departed in such a hurry. He cleaned out the bucket, filled it with the clear coat solution, and then wrung out the mop and started working in the back bedroom.

He moved quickly throughout the house, only stopping every now and then to check on Cass, who he had tied to the front entrance of the house. She would bark at the neighbors across the street or the cat next door. Tyrone only took an hour and a half to finish.

He cleaned everything up and left the window open so the air could help dry the floors faster. Still moving as fast as he could, he loaded up the car with everything that had to go back to the rental shop, untied Cass and took off.

Tyrone returned the rental equipment and then went home to call Jackie. He let her know that he was done and would be calling James to arrange for him to come by later to help get Jackie's things out of storage.

Jackie told Ty that she would call Carla and John and have them meet Jackie after work at Ty's house where they would all load up their cars with clothing and meet Ty and James at the Newton street place that evening.

Everything went as planned; by the time James and Ty made it to the house with the truck, Jackie, Carla, John, Jason, Ben and Caroline had all arrived. There was still plenty of daylight left and the floors were dry, so they began off-loading the truck and emptying the cars. Jackie asked the kids what they thought of their new home.

Ben spoke out: "This house looks haunted."

Everyone laughed and Jackie told Ben to be quiet, that he wouldn't know a haunted house if he'd been in one. Tyrone just looked at the boy strangely; Tyrone felt exactly the same way about the place, but Jackie did not want anyone talking like that around Caroline. Later, however, Tyrone told Ben that he had thought the same thing about the house the first time he saw it.

As night fell, the cold air once again penetrated the old structure. Ty closed the windows and they all left, heading to Ty's house to get the rest of Jackie's things, except for what she would need for work and the things the kids would need for school the following day.

Before returning to the Newton house, Jackie stopped and got food for the kids. They finished unpacking the truck and cars, locked up the old house and left.

Caroline fell fast asleep on the ride back to Ty's house while Jackie and Ty discussed plans for the remainder of the week.

When they pulled up in front of Ty's house, John, Carla, Jason and Ben were already there. Ben waited on the front steps and Jason, still not feeling comfortable about the living arrangements, stayed in the car. Jackie parked and Ty unbuckled Caroline's seat belt and carried her to the door. Ben took the keys out of Ty's hand and opened the door.

Jackie got out of the car and headed toward John's car to thank him and Carla for helping and to let Jason know that he would be staying at the old house on Newton Street and not anywhere else once they moved. He would also be helping to load the big things that had to come out of Ty's house and onto the rental truck.

"Why do I have to help when none of those things belong to me?" Jason argued.

Jackie had walked away from the car, but turned back around and delivered a tongue lashing to the boy.

"Do as you are told and start thinking about what you are going to do about school. You will still do as you're told until you turn 18 years of age," she finished. Jason didn't say another word as John and Carla bid good-bye to Jackie and drove off.

After putting Caroline to bed and saying good night to Ben, Ty met Jackie at the door as she was coming in.

"Is everything all right?" he asked.

Jackie managed a smile. "Let's go to bed," she said wearily.

They washed up and got into bed. Jackie rolled over toward Ty and thanked him for being so nice to the kids. Ty gave Jackie a kiss and they fell asleep holding one another.

Thursday morning Tyrone sat up in bed looking around as if he had overslept. He looked over at the clock—it was only five A.M. He lay back down knowing he would not be able to fall back to sleep.

Tyrone got up without waking Jackie or the kids. He went into the kitchen got something to drink and sat down. He picked up the note pad that listed the next two days' worth of chores. The new owners were moving into Ty's house on Saturday morning. It didn't seem like much time, considering all that he still had to pack. Help wouldn't come until the end of each day so he had to make every minute count.

Jackie came into the kitchen soon thereafter. The pressure associated with the move was mounting and Jackie's mood was a bit different; he could hear it in Jackie's voice as he bid her good morning. She said very little. The morning remained quiet mostly as Jackie and Ty got ready for their day. Ty knew that she was thinking about the move and his upcoming trip out of state. Ty had plans to drive the truck to Arizona on Saturday morning, so he could store all the things from his house there.

Soon, the kids were up. Caroline wanted to skip school. She wanted to help Tyrone pack and help pick up the truck from the rental store. She just wanted to go for a ride in it, she said. Tyrone let Caroline know that the truck would be there when she got home from school and that school was more important.

The rental store opened at seven and Jackie got Tyrone there just as the doors opened. The owner came out of the store and walked over to the truck. Tyrone said good-bye to Jackie and the kids and told Jackie not to worry. Nonetheless Tyrone had never driven a truck this big. The owner went over every detail of the massive vehicle to Tyrone, who made sure he took out insurance on the truck before he left the rental yard. This proved to be a good thing because Tyrone scratched and dented the top half of the truck while making a turn. He was so nervous he had forgotten about how long the truck was and forgot to turn out wide.

When Tyrone finally got home, he discovered that backing it into the driveway was just as difficult, especially with no ground guide. He called Jackie, told her what happened and she laughed.

"You had better get used to the truck in a hurry because it's a long way to Arizona." she warned.

"Thanks for reminding me," Ty replied, chuckling. "I love you and I'll pick up Caroline from school," he assured Jackie.

"Okay, but don't pick Caroline up in the truck," she joked.

They both laughed as she said good-bye.

The rest of that morning and half of the afternoon Tyrone spent loading the truck with one hundred banana boxes. He worked on emptying the back shed until it was time to pick up Caroline from school.

Caroline was glad to be home to help Ty load the truck although she just played in it most of the time. By the time Ben and Jason showed up, Ty was ready for another break and something to eat. Afterward they continued to load the truck until Jackie came home. By then it was dark and time to quit, but the little things were all loaded onto the truck.

When dinner was ready, they all sat down at the table and ate while watching TV. Tyrone told the kids to give their mom a hand with the dishes after dinner because he was going to bed early. Friday was the last day before he had to be out of his old house and he might have to work all night. Jason decided to stay the night since it was getting late. Before Tyrone went to bed he reminded Jackie not to stay up much later and to be sure the dog was fed and everything was locked up.

Friday morning, Ty asked Jackie what time she had come to bed. She told Ty it was right after he did, but Ty didn't remember a thing. Even Caroline got into the conversation.

"I came into the room to give you a kiss goodnight Daddy and you were already asleep," she said.

"Caroline, your Daddy is sorry all of this moving is taking a toll on me and I was very tired last night," he explained to Caroline.

Friday turned out to be a rougher day than expected. The truck was running out of room and people driving by began to stop and ask if Tyrone wanted to sell some of the items that still sat out on the driveway. Tyrone ended up giving the living room set to someone who stopped with a truck. Tyrone was becoming upset and the pressures of the move were starting to get to him.

The phone rang and he rushed into the house to answer it, hoping it was James, who was supposed to be bringing his brother Jack and another friend to help with the hot tub and gym equipment. Tyrone knew the boys couldn't help lift those things into the truck.

Instead, it was Jackie calling to see how everything was going and to let Ty know that she would be leaving work early to meet Nancy, a friend from out of town. Nancy wanted to take Jackie out shopping for a house warming gift for their new home. Nancy also wanted to see the place. Afterwards, they would pick up Caroline and the boys, and all come to Ty's house to help clean out the interior.

Finally James showed up with the promised help. He introduced Ty to his friend, Joe, and Ty told them how glad he was to see them. Right away the beer drinking started and continued for the next twenty minutes. Once they got started working however, things moved pretty quickly. Ty had to keep an eye on the time because he still had to make it to the title company to sign the house over to the new owners and get to the bank before it closed.

By the time Jackie arrived with Jason, Ben, Nancy and Caroline, the house was completely empty. With just a little time left before Ty had to go, he showed Jackie where he stored all of the cleaning material and showed Jason and Ben what he wanted them to do while he was gone. Even though it was growing dark, everyone kept right on working.

When Tyrone returned from the title company and bank, Jason and Ben had completed their assigned tasks. It was Friday night and they were ready to hit the streets. Tyrone paid Jason and Ben before they left, both happy, especially Jason; he hadn't expected that Ty would give them each one hundred dollars.

Ben ran into the house to tell Jackie that he was going out with Jason and they were going to stay the night at Carla's house.

Jackie came out to thank Ty for giving the boys money for their help, but she wasn't really pleased with the way James, Jack and Joe were carrying on with alcohol in front of the house while Nancy was there. Tyrone told the boys to go and have fun and to be careful. Jackie went back inside the house. But instead of talking to James about the group's behavior, Tyrone joined right in with them.

It was growing late. The girls had finished cleaning the house and it was time for Nancy to hit the road, as she had quite a drive ahead. Jackie walked Nancy out to the car and Ty thanked her for coming. They watched in silenced as Nancy drove off.

Ty was reluctant to go back inside the house with Jackie, because Ty knew she was going to be giving him an earful. Somehow Caroline had managed to fall asleep on the floor in the house. Tyrone picked up the child and carried her back outside to Jackie's car with Jackie following right behind them. Tyrone didn't say much because he knew Jackie was tired, angry and sad about the sale of Ty's house. Ty did ask Jackie if she was going to spend the night at the Newton Street house and she quickly responded, saying: "No way! That place is still a mess!" She said she was going to stay at the hotel down the street. Ty told Jackie that he would be along shortly after he paid off the rest of the help.

Tyrone did not make it to the hotel until three o'clock Saturday morning. He had to call the hotel to find out which room Jackie was staying in. Then he had a hard time waking Jackie up to answer the door. Tyrone left Cass in Jackie's car in the hotel parking lot.

The time passed by quickly Saturday morning. Jackie got Caroline ready to go while Ty found himself still in desperate need of rest. Jackie was very angry with Tyrone and was asking questions in a steady stream.

"Why did it take you half of the night to pay off those guys? What else were you all doing besides drinking?"

Ty didn't answer.

Jackie went to check out of the hotel while Caroline and Tyrone waited in the car with Cass. When Jackie returned, Ty asked Jackie to drop him off where he had left the truck.

"Why didn't you drive the truck here last night?" Jackie asked.

"There wasn't any room in the parking lot," Tyrone answered.

"Too bad! No, I won't drive you to the truck," she concluded.

Tyrone had to ride back to the Newton Street place with Jackie, who was meeting John, Carla, Jason and Ben for breakfast. They were all going to help Jackie get settled into the old house.

Tyrone knew he had to go—it was along ways to Arizona. So he kissed Caroline and wished everyone else good-bye, Tyrone got into his car which he had left at the Newton place the night before without saying a word to Jackie and left.

Tyrone drove to the place where in had parked the truck and pulled in behind the big U-Haul. Cass leaped out of the car and entered the truck when Jackie unexpectedly came roaring up and got out, leaving the engine running. She was yelling, pointing her finger at Ty's face and causing a scene, for someone to see if there was anyone watching. Ty was too tired to fight. He didn't even care, and simply gave Jackie some money and asked her to please get both cars back to the Newton house, where they would be safe while he was gone. Jackie didn't answer Tyrone; she simply got in the car, still crying, and left.

Tyrone got into the truck and watched out the side view mirror as Jackie disappeared down the road. Tyrone almost felt as if he would never see Jackie again. He started up the truck and then had to drive past the house he had just sold, taking one more look at the past while he kept on motoring up the road with tears running down his face.

It was no easy drive to Arizona. The truck had a five-speed transmission, the clutch pedal was longer than Tyrone's car's pedal and Tyrone could barely push this one to the floorboard. To add to the problem, the truck was one-and-a-half-tons overweight, making a tough drive all the more difficult.

Ty's friends in Arizona—Frank and Lucy—had gotten a little worried waiting for him to arrive at their house. When he finally arrived five hours behind schedule, the couple was much relieved.

Ty parked the truck and stepped out for a stretch, looking like hell, followed by Cass. Ty hugged Frank and Lucy. The old friends were too polite to make any comments on Ty's recent weight loss or other behavioral changes, but he could see the concern on their faces. Lucy instructed Frank to put Cass in the backyard and invited Ty to get the things he needed out of the truck and come inside. She showed him where to clean up, closed the girls' bedroom door and began preparing something for him to eat. Once Ty sat down to eat, Lucy encouraged him to get comfortable and catch up on some much needed rest. Frank and Ty would be engaged in some major unloading the following morning and a good night's sleep was crucial. Cass was fed and the three people went to bed.

Frank had everything worked out already for the following morning with regard to unloading the truck. He had reserved a storage area for Ty and everything on the truck fit right in as if it had been built to order.

By late Sunday afternoon after Ty spent time with Frank and Lucy's girls and Cass, he returned the truck to its drop-off destination and made arrangements to fly back to California the following day. He explained to Lucy and Frank that with the move happening so suddenly he had to get back to Monterey right away.

They understood. Frank assured Ty that he would see after all his things.

Cass was understandably confused when Ty brought her to the airport to check in on Monday afternoon. Frank and Lucy brought both of their girls to the airport to see Cass onto the plane. Their girls enjoyed Cass's short stay at their house and didn't want her to go. Cass was placed in a cage and sat with the rest of the bags to be loaded onto the plane.

It was a short flight home.

Chapter 4

Caroline couldn't wait to see Ty once his plane landed in Monterey. She hugged him and waited anxiously for Cass to make her appearance from the luggage department. Caroline admitted that she couldn't wait to move to a climate, with her own swimming pool.

"The day will come Caroline, we'll just have to wait and see," Ty said.

Jackie simply stood by and waited until Caroline's excitement was somewhat spent. She still hadn't gotten over the way she and Ty parted ways. Since Jackie didn't hear from him while he was gone, they didn't have much to say to one another. They did manage to give each other a perfunctory hug before barking could be heard. Caroline watched as the airline employees opened Cass's cage and rushed to give her beloved pet a big hug and kiss.

The group walked back to the car and Jackie drove everyone to the Newton Street house. Once they arrived, Ty chained up Cass as there wasn't any fencing around the house. Ty then walked the grounds to get an idea of what he was going to need to clean up the outside. Layers of spider webs and dirt covered the house, making the paint look dull. Getting all the weeds cut down and all the trash hauled away was going to be another big job.

The sun was about to set when Jackie called out to Ty to come inside and eat. He was not only hungry, but tired and ready for some sleep. After making sure the cars were locked up and the suitcase had been brought inside he was ready to eat. The interior of the old house was attractive. Jackie and the kids, however, had done a surprisingly good job of decorating the place.

After dinner, Ty took a bath and then checked on Cass one more time before watching a little TV and falling asleep. Soon thereafter, Jason and Ben came home while Jackie and Caroline slept on the floor with the TV still on.

Tyrone got up off the couch, which converted into a bed, and Jackie and Caroline slept there, while the boys went straight to bed, leaving Tyrone awake and alone, listening to a series of unfamiliar sounds within and without the house. Since Cass wasn't barking Ty was barely aware of them. Eventually, he turned off the TV and fell asleep on the floor.

The sun shone brightly through the house the next morning, as not all of the windows had curtains. It was a hectic morning, with everyone vying to use the lone small bathroom in order to wash up for work and school. Jackie and Ty still hadn't spoken much to each other since his return home. When Jackie and Caroline emerged from the bathroom, Tyrone had already washed up in the kitchen sink and had breakfast prepared. Everyone sat down and had a little bite to eat while Ty got Caroline's school lunch ready.

When Tyrone walked back into the house after seeing Jackie and the kids off to work and school, it felt as if he had been living there for sometime. He fell right into a routine, cleaning up the kitchen and bathroom.

Just as Ty was about to head outside to feed Cass and rearrange the items in the small storage, Steve, his brother-in-law, showed up at the door to see how the remodeling turned out. As they started talking and began looking the place over, Steve commented wryly that the house looked as if it sat atop of a graveyard.

"What a coincidence!" Tyrone replied, telling Steve about Ben's similar remark regarding the house.

Tyrone then mentioned to Steve that he had experienced some uncomfortable sensations about this place himself. This inspired Steve to share some things that he had experienced a few years earlier.

"When I was 15, 16 years old, I worked at a golf course as a cart boy and during the week at night, there would invariably be a cart broke down somewhere on the course and I'd have to go out in the dark to retrieve it. Well, one night I got a call from the owner's son who lived by the 13th tee box—through the farmland, across the river, down a long dirt road. Anyway, the son would always call me and have me bring him food and cigarettes, but it had always been during the day, so I didn't mind going. But this was night! I tried as hard as I could to convince him that I couldn't come. But the son insisted that I get him what he wanted. I was young and afraid of losing my job so I got in the greens' keeper's cart, got the things he asked for and headed out in the dark toward his house. It was tough getting down that dirt road because of the big German shepherd that would bite at my leg as I wove back and forth to keep it from getting a good bite off of me. As I approached the house, I noticed it was well lit with candles inside and out. I didn't think much of it. I got out of the cart and went up to the door and called out to the son. But there was no answer."

Ty interrupted. "Where did the dog go?"

"The dog would only chase me so far down the dirt road each time I came to the house. Dog didn't belong to him anyway."

Steve continued. "I knocked harder on the door and still no answer. The door wasn't closed all the way so I opened it and went in calling him by name. I turned to the left and entered the living room. There straight in front of me was a large figure, and the son kneeling down in front of it with candles burning all around him. At first it was hard to make out what was going on until I took one step closer. There I could see the horns on the massive figure, as well as his large pointed teeth. It scared the shit out of me, Ty. I dropped what I had in my hands and ran out of the house. I got into the cart drove back up the dirt road dodging the German shepherd, over the river I went and through the golf course to the cart house. I never looked back. My parents were already there waiting for me; they came at a certain time every night to pick me up form work. I couldn't talk. I was speechless, I was out of breath, traumatized and to this day my parents don't know what happened to me that night."

Ty whistled. "Steve, that was some heavy shit my man; did anyone ever confront that freak?" Ty asked.

"My older brother did, but there was no resolution. That creep was so far gone it was scary. When I was going through a break-up with my first wife, I drank a lot. I'd go out in my backyard and get some fresh air, and I'd look and see something in the dark—a figure. At first I would go back in the house because I was frightened by it, and when I got the nerve to go back out and walk towards it, it would dissolve right into thin air."

"What else happened?" Tyrone asked.

"I could feel something following close behind me when I would walk around outside the house, so I would pray and spread holy water all around saying my Hail Marys. I'm Catholic, you know," Steve added.

"Well it looks like I'll have to start doing some of the same things, Catholic or not," Tyrone replied. Both Steve and Ty chuckled as they walked back toward his truck.

Nonetheless Steve believed that Ty should trust his feeling regarding this old Newton house, which didn't make Ty feel any more relaxed about being there by himself. Ty held a fist up high in the air and shook it as Steve drove away.

As Ty walked towards the shed in the back yard, he was in an emotional frame of mine, but couldn't help laughing uneasily at what Steve and he had discussed. He believed every word Steve had said about the place.

"Hey Cass," Ty called out as he petted and unchained her.

Ty began rearranging and moving the empty boxes and the things that weren't going to be needed into the shed. Suddenly, an unidentifiable, unsettling feeling began to grip him. He also noticed Cass's behavior was a bit unusual. The dog was sniffing all around the shed as if she was trying to catch up with something. Whatever it was, Cass appeared to have it on the run. Ty finished up with the shed and made himself some lunch.

After lunch Ty called Jackie at work to see how her day was going and ask if she wanted him to look for the boys after picking up Caroline from school. Jackie replied that she would get the boys after she got off from work.

But she did ask Ty to set out some meat for dinner and make sure Caroline completed all of her homework before she watched any TV.

After assuring Jackie that he would see to it, Ty hung up the phone and cleaned up the little mess he had made before returning outside. Ty didn't have much time left before he had to drive across town to pick up Caroline. Still, he decided to wash down the back side of the house which would make a big improvement in its appearance.

Tyrone locked everything up and told Cass to get in the car before heading off to pick up Caroline from school. Once he made the decision, Ty couldn't wait to get back and finish washing the dirt off the house, wanting to get it all done before Jackie got home from work. He put out some snacks for Caroline and they got started on her homework. With that task completed, Ty went out back to wash down the house.

When Jackie and the boys got home, they commented on how bright the yellow paint on the house had turned out.

"What a big difference," Jackie marveled.

Ty was pleased to hear Jackie speak that way; it had been awhile since they had spoken to one another in a friendly manner.

After cleaning up outside, Ty cleaned himself up, entered the kitchen and wrapped his arms around Jackie's waist from behind. She turned around and responded with a hug and kiss.

After dinner, Ty cleaned up the kitchen and once the kids fell asleep, he and Jackie decided to go out and have a few drinks. Jackie and Ty were using a lot of crack cocaine they preferred to smoke it. After leaving the bar on their way back to the Newton house they stopped at a friend's house and scored some crack.

When they returned to the old house on Newton Street, it was still fairly early but it seemed later because of the stillness and darkness in the area surrounding the place. There was neither a sound to be heard nor a light to be seen.

Once they got inside the house Jackie and Tyrone were getting high and enjoying one another when they became aware of strange noises. Of course, with one's mind altered, a lot of things can happen to change one's perceptions and thinking.

Ty lay wide awake later on that night listening to a pounding sound that seemed to erupt from the strange house and the footsteps running back and forth underneath him where he laid inside the old house long after Jackie had fallen asleep. He couldn't pinpoint either the nature of the noises or its source but they were clearly coming from somewhere under, in or around the house.

As morning grew near, Ty continued listening to the pounding and the running sounds as he drifted in and out of a fitful sleep. He was relieved when the boys, then Caroline, got up and started preparing for school.

Jackie lay still, trying to squeeze in a few more minutes of rest. Ty moved closer and gave her a few kisses. "Wake up sleeping beauty."

"Don't push it," Jackie replied laughing. "Did you sleep well?"

"I slept like a baby," he lied.

Jackie knew that wasn't the truth merely by looking at his eyes. He lay mostly on the floor, the pad they were laying on, not being big enough for two adults.

"Well," she decided, "you should be able to get some rest after me and the kids leave." When Jackie and the kids finally did leave, Ty decided to postpone cleaning up the mess the kids had made in the kitchen. Instead, he simply sat back in the chair and continued thinking about the weird noises that had haunted him all night. He wondered if it had been his imagination. Eventually, exhausted, he fell asleep in the chair for two hours, until the phone rang, waking him up.

It was Jackie, calling to report what a nice time she'd had.

"I love you," she said.

"I love you too, baby." He said good-bye, hung up the phone then cleaned the kitchen and fed Cass. The house was so small it didn't take long to straighten up.

It was hard for Ty to stop thinking about Jackie's conversation. He knew what it meant; they indulged in each other so well on that crack cocaine, when he could sit still and not look out any windows. That's was how he knew it was party time, but he also understood that there were things that had to be done around the house to make it safe before they started back indulging in bad habits.

With this on his mind Ty began checking over the house very carefully for possible means of entry. He began sealing up the attic and reinforcing the back door, making it almost impossible to breach. He was so into the various tasks that he didn't even realize that lunchtime had passed. He had to hurry as it was already time to pick up Caroline from school.

He took Cass along for the ride, as Caroline was always excited when Cass was in the car. Ty knew that Cass and Caroline would keep each other busy on the way back to the house. He did not want Caroline to sense any of the concerns he was having about this old house on Newton Street.

Chapter 5

With each passing day, a haunting sensation crept like a shadow into Tyrone's senses, his imagination magnifying each perception. There was a constant rattling of the windows even when no wind was blowing. But the locks on the kitchen windows and bathroom window were the only things that really concerned him—they were locked tight, and nothing could get through without him knowing it still, this constant rattling unsettled him. Screws can come loose from powerful vibrations. The locks, he decided, would eventually need to be replaced.

Ty was on full alert, barely sleeping at night. Wednesday, Thursday and Friday nights of the first week were pretty much the same. He and Jackie were on a roll, getting high each of those nights into the early morning.

Jackie and the kids were barely able to get up each day in order to go to school and work. Ty's days weren't any better. He was trying to maintain but was, in fact, becoming increasingly paranoid. The noises now came from the windows, cabinets and closets. At times, it seemed to ooze up from under the house itself. He even tried to rationalize the phenomenon, thinking it might be the activity of an animal. But in the end he simply could not accept the idea that an animal was the ultimate answer to everything happening around the house. He knew there had to be something more.

By Saturday morning, however the house had settled down and Ty was feeling a bit relieved because he wouldn't have to drive across town to pick up Caroline from school later that day. He was much too tired, and all he could think about was trying to catch up on some rest.

Jason and Ben had spent the night over at a friend's house and Ty wasn't expecting them home anytime soon. Jackie lay on the sofa with Caroline huddled next to her.

Despite his exhausted state, Ty got up to feed Cass and use the bathroom, checking to make sure that Jackie had set the alarm clock before laying back down. She had been working the swing shift at a five star restaurant part time over the past two years, and it would be her first weekend back on the job after taking some time off.

Ty never heard the alarm clock ring or Jackie and Caroline get up. He was finally awakening by Jackie on her way out the door. He looked up at her and muttered "Be careful," as she left in a hurry. He didn't even try to get up. Instead, he glanced at Caroline, who was watching TV, and then curled up and went back to sleep.

Jason and Ben finally showed up with some friends and proceeded to parade in and out of the house. At one point, Caroline put on some shoes and joined them outside. Then Cass started making a little more noise than usual. In fact she was barking angrily as if being attacked.

Ty hurried outside to discover that Jason, Ben, Caroline and their friends were nowhere in sight.

He found Cass barking into the screen covering a vent that led to the area under the house. Ty commanded her to stop barking, but she would not stop. Bending down to see what was causing her excitement, he peered through the screen and found himself staring at a truly unworldly creature.

"Shit! What the hell is that, Cass?" he blurted, almost as if he expected an answer. The thing was black and four legged, with a very long and undulating tail. It was quite large, had wide square shoulders and the chest of a human. Its pointed face looked to be an unnatural co-mingling of animal, human and rarified evil. The creature possessed large, glowing yellow eyes. Overall its face looked something like a large cat, perhaps a black panther. Tyrone had surely never seen anything like it.

The animal turned and began walking away from him, but Tyrone continued to stare intently as it peered back at him over its shoulder, staring directly into Tyrone's eyes for a few seconds that seemed more like minutes.

"Oh my God," Ty mumbled, his tongue and brain in vapor lock.

The monstrosity then walked toward what seemed like an endless dark hall, until Tyrone could no longer see it. The darkness transformed the area beneath the house into a sort of netherworld where space and time seemed different, somehow.

Between his encounter with the creature and the disappearance of the kids, Tyrone panicked, calling out to the boys and Caroline.

The boys, their friends and Caroline all came running, and before Ty could even speak, he was being told all at once about the strange things that the kids found in the barn. The objects included a photo album and a newspaper article about a boy who had killed himself long ago. Ty was almost out of breath as he told the kids to stay away from that barn and not to go back inside it ever again. He then took the newspaper article from Jason, and told Caroline to go back inside the house and watch TV until it was time for dinner. Ty then told Jason and Ben that their friends could stay a little while longer, so the boys went inside, to play computer games. Ty decided not to mention anything about what he had seen under the house.

Shaken, he took the article into the kitchen and began reading it while preparing dinner. The headline read: "Boy Hurt In Blast Shoots Self Dead (June 25, 1923—Associated Press) Monterey, CA. Joseph Hillzer, 8, Commits Suicide After Painful Injury." Joseph, it seems, was a precocious child, having already passed the eighth grade examination at his tender age. On that June day in 1923 the 8-year-old found a dynamite cap near his house that had been left behind by a grading crew. It exploded, leaving him badly wounded. He managed to make it home with his sister, trying to stop his bleeding. Unable to face disfigurement for the rest of his life, the boy went into the house, retrieved a .32 caliber revolver from his mother's dresser and shot himself through the heart.

The sun was about to set and dinner was almost ready. Caroline came into the kitchen to help set the table and tell Jason and Ben that dinner was ready.

The boys' friends left and they soon joined Ty and Caroline at the kitchen table. The kids could sense that Ty was still troubled, probably thinking about the barn, so they kept very quiet while eating. Eventually, however Ty's curiosity overcame the silence as he began asking question about the barn. Jason did most of the talking, describing in detail the interior of the old structure, describing the stairs leading up to the second floor. Ty's anxiety grew as he visualized what Jason was describing.

"Were there a lot of spider webs in that barn?" Ty asked Caroline.

Her eyes grew large in response.

"Yes! And one almost touched me" she answered quickly. "Everything was really old."

Ty knew Caroline did not like spiders and would definitely think more than twice before going near that barn again. He then made sure the kids understood that the barn was totally off limits.

"There's no telling what could be in that barn," he explained.

Everyone agreed there would be no more going in that barn.

After dinner Jason and Ben went back into their room and Caroline helped Ty clean up the kitchen and feed Cass. Ty then cleaned Caroline up and read her a story before bedtime. She finally fell asleep and several hours later Jackie walked into the house. It startled Ty who had dozed off with the TV on and didn't hear her car pull into the driveway.

He popped right up, eager to tell Jackie what had taken place earlier in the day. The story of what had happened with Cass, the beast beneath the house and the children's' discovery of the news article about the dead child spilled out all at once.

Jackie's reaction was simple. Not only did she not believe a word he said, she thought it was ridiculous—and probably the result of overindulgence in their bad habit.

"Have you been getting high on your own?" she accused. 'I hope you haven't discussed any such wild notions around Caroline or the boys?" she added with real menace in her eyes.

Ty became frustrated at her incredulity but Jackie simply refused to hear any more of what he had to say and stalked off to check on the boys. Both Jason and Ben were fast asleep. She turned off their TV and closed the door to their room.

Ty made one last effort to sell Jackie by showing her the newspaper article about the dead boy. She read it, but remained unconvinced.

Ty decided to pour himself a glass of wine and offered one to Jackie as she undressed and got into the sofa bed with Caroline.

She barely finished half the glass before falling asleep, and Ty left her alone.

Soon, he was high all by himself. That night Tyrone's guard was down. As a result, whatever force seemed to dwell within this house, actually drove him outside directly into the still, dark night. He felt as if the house was about to be invaded, as if some kind of unseen gang was surrounding the house. Cass barked like a tornado was headed over the horizon. Suddenly, Ty heard a rumbling, basso voice command Cass to "Shut up!" There had been string of break-in attempts at his last house, and he feared that someone might be trying to do the same thing here.

Ty was still stone which only amplified the sense of evil and anxiety surrounding the house. Whatever he had disturbed in this old house was taking full advantage of his existing paranoia and weakness. He was beginning to wish it were a gang of things moving in on the house—especially given that cat-thing he'd encountered beneath the house.

Ty was torn with guilt. He wanted so badly to go back into the house to warn and protect Jackie and the kids. But he could not pull himself sufficiently together to do so.

Desperate, engulfed in panic, he hoisted a big rock and heaved it through the front window. Following the great crash of breaking glass, he waited for some kind of reaction, but nothing came, not even a light in a nearby home. It seemed to Ty as if he and Cass were the only ones left alive on Newton Street.

Suddenly, Jackie appeared in the doorway, angry after being wakened out of a dead sleep to the sound of glass crashing to the floor. She began yelling.

"What in the hell is wrong with you?" she demanded. "Come in the house!"

Ty refused to re-enter the house, insisting instead that Jackie check on the boys to see if they were all right. She stormed back towards the boys' room, as Ty walked tentatively up the steps and peeked through the front door to make sure she had done as he commanded.

When he heard her returning to the front door, he frantically attempted to explain what he had done, but Jackie interrupted him, fury flashing in her eyes. "The boys are fine," she said through gritted teeth. "I cannot believe you threw a damn rock through our window!" Without another word she turned on her heel and went back to bed, leaving Ty standing silently in the doorway.

He spent the rest of the night guarding the broken window which he had taped up and blocked with some cardboard. He sat awhile, and then walked through the house, broken glass crunching under his shoes, trying to put all of this together—the uneasy feeling, the rattling windows and floors, the creature under the house and the significance of the dead boy in the article.

This house brought so much fear into Ty's heart that he felt the need to protect himself constantly. He started carrying either a knife or a baseball bat while walking around inside the house. However, he soon realized that if his suspicion about the house were correct, a knife or a baseball bat would not be any help.

Ty could no longer sit in any one place for long. A noise coming from the closet would attract his attention and he would have to check it out. He would stand next to the closet door trying to make out the sounds that drifted constantly from that location. He slowly opened the door and got the shit scared out of him by an enormous black spider that dropped from the darkness and dangled in front of his face.

"Damn," he exclaimed, closing the door quickly while trying to convince himself that he had not seen anything. He did not want to remember anything about it.

Fatigue was setting in quickly.

Every time he looked at something, it began to assume the form of the thing he had seen under the house. It seemed to be able to grow or shrink right before his eyes. Still, he struggled to stay awake. Tyrone drifted in and out of sleep until the sun lit up the room.

It wasn't long before the sun filled the house. Jackie was up and making coffee. It was Sunday morning so she would be going to church and visiting with family before heading to work. Ben and Jason would also be rising early to catch a ride into town while Caroline remained asleep.

Ty left the chair to lie down next to Caroline where it was much more comfortable. Even though he was tired enough to sleep the day away, he could not. He had to make some kind of arrangement to get the window fixed before Jackie returned home that evening, but didn't see it as a problem as long as he could get hold of James. Ty had noticed a few large pieces of glass on the side of the mysterious barn that he could use to replace the broken window.

He lay there thinking over the incidents that took place the previous night, wondering if the boys had heard anything. What was he going to say to them and would Jackie even speak to him before she left for work that morning? He would soon find out.

Jackie was finally ready to leave. Ben and Jason were rushing through the house, picking through the cabinets and refrigerator, putting food in a bag to take with them.

Caroline, awakened by all of the commotion, got out of bed to say good-bye to mom. Jackie hugged and kissed Caroline and pointed at the floor.

"There is glass all over, be careful," she warned glaring at Ty.

The boys emerged from the kitchen hassling one another. Jason hurried out the door without saying anything. Ben, though, gave Caroline a hug and said to Ty, "Keep an eye on the house." Then he chuckled and left.

Ty asked Jackie to say a prayer for him; he needed it.

Jackie replied, "All I know is, you better take care of things around this house and make sure Caroline is washed, fed and looked after all day." She then closed the door behind her. Caroline went to the window to wave good-bye. Ty reached for the phone and called James, letting the phone ring until his friend answered.

"Hey, James, this is Ty. I need another favor from you. I broke out the front window at this Newton house and I was wondering if you could come over and fix it for me."

"How did you do that?" James asked.

"I don't want to go into detail over the phone; I'll tell you about it when you get here." Ty answered.

"I'll be there before lunchtime."

"Thanks!" Ty hung up the phone then laid back and released a sigh of relief.

Caroline was ready to eat so Ty immediately jumped up as if full of energy. He fed her and then let her soak and play in the tub for a while, using that time to vacuum up the very small pieces of glass from the broken window and get the house back in order.

James showed up right before lunch and started removing the remains of broken glass from the window frame. Caroline wanted to help.

"It's too dangerous, Caroline. You could get cut." James warned.

"What could I do?" she asked.

"Would you like to play in the car with Cass?" Ty suggested, hoping to distract her.

"Yes," she replied. Playing in the car was Caroline's favorite thing to do. Ty unchained Cass and showed Caroline what she would not be allowed to touch inside the car.

In the meantime, James, eagerly waiting to hear what had happened, walked toward the barn, Ty right behind him. As they examined the glass that would replace the shattered window. Ty explained that he had thrown a rock through the window, and why. As crazy as it may have sounded, James took him seriously though he still laughed. Then he finished replacing the window and everyone but Cass went inside and ate lunch.

After lunch, James reminded Ty to be sure to call him ahead of time when he was ready to clean up the property. He promised to recruit a couple more guys to help out, believing that it would take a full weekend to finish.

Ty thanked James again.

James said good-bye to Caroline and told his friend to be careful and to slow down. Tyrone watched him drive away and then noticed that there was a full construction crew building a house and a telephone repair man high up on a pole, working right across the street.

It was a Sunday afternoon and the workers seemed strangely out of place. Ty wondered where in the hell they had come from. Ty was still suffering the aftereffects of the booze and drugs, and it showed. He had been paying little attention to his surroundings, and continued to ignore James' advice to slow down. Things deteriorated throughout the rest of the day and late into the night.

Jason, Ben and a friend came home. It was late, and Ty was expecting Jackie at any moment.

"Did anything strange happen while we were gone?" Ben wondered. He had attempted to call home all evening following a bad premonition regarding the old house. He had had a feeling that all kinds of nasty things were going to break loose. Ty then told the boys about a conversation he had had with the spirits and demons, and what they looked like. "This took place right before you got here," he began.

The boys laughed, but Ben had lots of questions.

"How did you come to be conversing with these demons, Ty?" he asked.

The boys sat forward on their bed waiting to hear more.

"It was during the day," Ty began. "Something scared the hell out of me and ran me out of the house into the street again. This time people were working outside and I was carrying a butcher knife in my hand. Before I realized what was happening, I'm in the middle of the road looking like I'm crazy."

Ben, Jason and their friend started laughing, but their uncertainly was obvious.

"All of a sudden Caroline calls for me from inside the house," Tyrone continued.

The boys stopped laughing and listened in suspense.

"Here I am, still frightened, standing in the street thinking that this was it. What in the fuck was I going to do? I'm still thinking that I can't just stand here wasting time. Something was happening to Caroline inside the house. I could hear her calling. I was ready to fight for her life. But I was afraid to go back into the house by myself. So I hollered 'Can I get some help?'"

That startled the boys.

"There was a telephone repair man who came down from the pole across the street. He looked at me and I stared back at him. Neither he nor I said a word to each other. The next thing he knew I was rushing back toward this house with the knife still in my hand. When I found Caroline in the bathroom I realized that she'd been calling so I would check to make sure she was clean enough to get off the toilet.

"Now, as I was helping her up, I began wondering about what the telephone repairman must be thinking or doing. I decided to pretend like I had something to show Caroline outside, so the repairman would see that everything was okay with her. "His head just shook. He looked at me, and climbed back up the pole. I was sure the repairman thought that I was crazy."

Jason interrupted me and asked, "Where was Caroline when you first ran out the front door?"

"She must have already gone to the bathroom; she was watching TV. But I didn't even notice. I was too busy running for the door."

The boys laughed again. Hard.

"It bothered me, being chased out of the house for the second time. I couldn't stand it. I knew then that it was time to regroup. That was when—and why—I decided to confront whatever was in this house. I waited until Caroline fell asleep and I started trying to make contact with the spirit or spirits or whatever they are. I thought maybe it, or them, did not like me smoking dope in the house. So I made a promise out loud to refrain from it. 'Come out and talk!' I demanded. I knew the knife I had been carrying around couldn't hurt whatever inhabited this place. I just wanted them to show themselves. I gave up checking on the windows but they were driving me crazy. I continued to demand to see and speak to whatever was responsible for the things going on in and around this house.

"Before I knew it, I was in a full out loud argument with myself. 'But I fixed it up,' I insisted, pointing to the remodeling I had accomplished—as if my renovations would impress these otherworldly invaders. The spirits and I went at it. That was when the welcoming committee showed up. A bunch of black human old heads, no bodies, with large yellow eyes suddenly appeared in the house. Soon, beings of all types and sizes showed up."

The boys sat quietly now, listening intently as Ty continued to talk about the events of that night.

"One being that I remember particularly well was a female demon. It had the appearance of a black cat. I instinctively knew it was a female. Bitch stared straight at me! I was half expecting this damn cat to jump directly at me but I just stared back at it. My attention was focused on that female cat, speaking directly to it. I even attempted to explain that my work on the damn house had probably saved it from being torn down, which would've left them no place to live. All that I had done was to upgrade the place. If they didn't like the changes—sealing up the attic, the vents, under the floor space, and other things I had done for protections—I would undo them. 'Let's just share the damn place!' I was yelling. The heat was on! I could smell it. The tension in the house was heavy," Tyrone told the boys.

He was getting worked up all over again. He needed to calm down. Jackie would be coming home soon and he did not want to wake up Caroline.

"I made a deal with the spirits," Ty told the boys. "I vowed that I would not carry a knife or baseball bat around in the house if they would stop rattling the windows and trying to run me out of the house. If the spirits and I are going to live in this house together then we have to give one another respect." The boys, nodded in understanding.

"I showed strength by telling the spirits that I would fight them or destroy the house if I had to. I told the spirits that Jackie thought I was going crazy. As ridiculous as all this may sound, I think things were resolved tonight," he told the boys.

Jason, Ben and their friend just shook their heads and chuckled, nervously overwhelmed by Tyrone's story.

"We hope you do have everything under control," Ben responded, and the boys all agreed.

As Ty walked out of their room he asked the boys to keep down the noise. Jackie's car was just then pulling into the driveway.

Tyrone opened the door to let her in. They were both very tired and slept well that night.

Monday morning everyone got up and prepared for school and work as usual. Ty was still tired but helped prepare lunches while the kids ate breakfast. It wasn't long before everyone but Ty was gone and the house was quiet again. He decided to go back to sleep.

Two hours later Ty was awakened by the sound of running bath water. He soon discovered a trail of water emerging from the bathroom that led out the front door. Ty took a good look, sighed and then said simply; "Good morning, spirits."

Tyrone got up to let the forces in the house know he was aware of their activity and was not bothered by them at the moment. He attempted to initiate communication with the spirits once again, requesting that they knock on the wall if they understood. He finally convinced them to create a sound—a thump in the bathroom. He started to head toward the bathroom at that time, but suddenly felt uneasy and decided to ignore it. Instead, he went outside to check on Cass, putting fresh water in her bowl and feeding her. Everything seemed normal outside, but it had gotten a little over-the-top inside the house, so Tyrone dressed and left a little earlier than usual to pick up Caroline from school.

When they returned, he did not expect to hear the splashing of bath water, but he did—it was the spirits, taking a bath.

Ty sat Caroline down and explained that the ghostly phenomena were benevolent spirits and that she should not be frightened. He put together a little snack and when they sat down to eat, the conversation about their so-called "friends" continued.

"Caroline, Dad doesn't really know what is going on other than we are sharing this house with people that once lived here, but are here now as spirits."

"Ok dad, I won't be afraid. Can I go outside and play?" Caroline asked.

"Yes you may."

They finished their snacks and tidied up the place before Caroline went outside to play.

Ty decided to remain inside, watch a little TV and relax. He believed his bond with the spirits was becoming keener by the minute. There was no getting anything by him! Ty knew where they were at all times but did not know what they were planning to do, or if they even had a plan.

A little later, things quieted down and Ty began to feel that everything was cool. He decided to fire up some crack and blow the smoke out the door. He became a little paranoid of course and repeatedly went outside to check on Caroline. She was always fine. Ty sat down on porch and thought about the situation, "I can't believe this. Bunk this, I live here, I'm high, so what? I did not smoke in the house; I did not break any promises. So why should I be scared? This is what I do."

He sat there defiantly for a few more minutes until Caroline decided that she did not want to play outside any more and joined Ty on the porch before they returned back into the house together.

It was like a spectral circus in there, sights so amazing that they actually decided to sit and watch. Neither of them ever imagined that spirits could take so many baths in one day. They saw the bathroom door opening and closing and heard the spirits walking from the bathroom out the front door and back inside, trailing water as they went. The house was in full use by the supernatural tenants. Ty and Caroline sat and watched this haunted bath house scene until the last spirit emerged from the bathroom and headed outside. The pair learned a lot during this time, deciding that a good experience could come out of this.

Tyrone told himself again that he must fight the fear.

Eventually, it was time to prepare dinner. Caroline came into the kitchen to help. Shortly after, Ben and Jason come home from school. Caroline immediately ran out of the kitchen into the boys' room, and Tyrone heard her telling Ben and Jason about the spirits. Jason scoffed and told her to get out of their room. The boys were more interested in playing their new Nintendo video game for now, than listening to fanciful tales from a little sister.

Tyrone called to Caroline to come finish setting the table. By the time dinner was ready the kids were hungry and ate enthusiastically while Ty fed Cass.

The phone rang; it was Jackie wanting to know how dinner had gone. She got to leave the restaurant early on Monday nights and wanted Ty to make sure Caroline was in bed early and that the boys turned off the Nintendo before she got home. Ty understood. Monday nights were their normal party nights. However, they were in for a surprise that Monday night.

Chapter 6

When Jackie arrived home, everything was exactly the way she wanted it. Ty had pulled out the bed and they were soon laying on it having a good time getting high. That was when the spirits showed up in full force and staged a light show.

The spectacular effects had Ty reacting out loud, "That's RAD!"

There were dark bats and unearthly things draped in white lace winging around the house. The chandelier started dimming and transformed into a crystal-encrusted skeletal head, its eyes blazing and its prismatic teeth smiling in a display of male volatility. Ty was so high and so into the visuals that he missed the most significant part of the party.

Jackie's doubts about the house being haunted were now out the window. All along she had thought that Ty was either crazy or high because of all the strange things he had been describing. Now, she was bug-eyed with fright and suddenly understood why Ty was responding so vocally that night. Also sounds once again emanated from under the floorboards.

Ty, however, seemed in tune with this world of darkness. His imagination grew increasingly keen and the more he saw, the wilder his fancies ran.

Eventually, the spectral effects started wearing off like the closing seconds of a fireworks exhibition but for Ty the night was developing perceptions that seemed more real than ever.

I'm living with the dead, Ty said to himself.

The spirits are setting me up to take over my family, Ty decided. Pretending, making Ty believe that everything was okay. They were one, big happy family, he had thought, living all together. Now he knew they were watching him and Jackie have intercourse while they were getting high. He fantasized and made jokes, knowing the dead were looking on.

"Spirits, want some of this?" he'd ask, slapping Jackie across the thigh. "I'm going to let the spirits have part of this woman," he would tease Jackie, who said nothing. She only stared.

Ty started worrying a little about whether he was still in control. He didn't know what would happen if he lost control, but felt that with faith and the belief he had in himself and the Higher Power he would survive this night. But as soon as he thought of the Higher Power he became disturbed and uncomfortable and got out of bed to look outside the window. The house seemed as of it had a shield over it, so nobody could see or hear what went on inside. The neighborhood seemed dead and everything connected to the living was still and quiet. But as for the dead, Ty could hear their invisible cars pulling up, doors closing, and spirits laughing and chatting as they strolled into the house.

Small creatures played in the yard. Ty guessed they were the kids and pets of the spirits attending the party. And what a party! Despite the fact that most everything was invisible, there were still plenty of shadows and the light show continued.

Eventually, Ty got back into bed with Jackie, where he was stuck, couldn't move and found himself completely naked. He wanted to do it some more but was overwhelmed by the feeling he had, like the spirits were about to overtake both him and the entire night in a major way. Ty tried to get things going but Jackie was too shook up. She had just been lying there, quite and staring. Jackie had seen more than she could handle. She remained totally still and was seriously tripping. But Ty was suddenly acting like a hound dog. Just like the living dead that filled the house, lurking and plotting over her body.

Soon, morning grew near and Jackie finally started to fall asleep, but not Tyrone. Even though his eyes were tired from staring into the dark he knew he would be safer in daylight. So Tyrone waited until the sun came up, and then dropped off to sleep.

He awoke later in the day.

"Caroline, when did mommy leave?" he asked.

"A few minutes ago," she answered.

After waiting a little longer, Ty called Jackie at work. She told him she had phoned in and taken the morning off and wouldn't be working at the restaurant tonight. Jason and Ben caught the bus to school and of course Caroline was still home.

Tyrone attempted discussing the events of the previous night but Jackie refused.

When she came home that night, Jackie was silent. Ty decided not to press the issue of last night's spook festival. But they did talk a little after dinner, after the boys went to their room and Caroline took a bath. They were cleaning the kitchen and before the pipe made its increasingly regular appearance, Jackie said, "It's best to stay sober." Ty agreed. After the previous night, who wouldn't?

Things were quiet but uneasy around the house until Thursday when Jackie called from work and informed Ty that she'd had a palm reading.

Jackie reported the palmist's diagnosis: a young spirit was hanging out at their house but he was harmless. It seems Jackie had experienced a ghost sighting—she saw the same young boy whose suicide was reported in the old newspaper clipping the kids found in the barn. The boy had been the host of the previous evening's ghost party.

"A real live ghost?" Tyrone replied. "I didn't see the young boy. Why didn't you tell me?"

She didn't answer.

"Wow! Hope you have a good day," he said, and hung up the phone. Jackie had gotten a personal introduction to one of the things that dwelled within the old house on Newton Street. No telling what the young spirit might have done that night, Ty thought, remembering his sexual taunts of the night before.

His mind started working overtime. There was now a young boy's ghost, as well as a weird animal under the house that he knew of for certain. Maybe the animal was the kid's damned pet. Ty now felt sure that whatever was prowling within the old house was nothing like the intruders he'd encountered at his previous residence. Those punks wouldn't have survived an encounter with the thing he had seen under the house anyway. Now he understood that this was a serious situation. He should have packed up their things and left this house. The sight of such a strange beast and knowing that it lived under their own house would've sent most people packing. However, Ty had sold his previous house and Jackie and the kids had no other place to go.

So they remained.

If Ty were to report this to the authorities, no one would believe a damn word. His brain was working frantically and he just hoped it wouldn't explode before he got to the bottom of the strange goings-on at the old Newton house.

He had already spent a lot of time in the previous few days and nights thinking over the situation. By trying to juggle the responsibilities of the move and an unstable lifestyle, he had landed in a bad situation one that would force him to confront his current lifestyle. Things had been working out well for them as a family unit in those past few days and Ty kept busy as best he could.

Thursday night was no different from the previous few nights, with sounds still rising up from underneath the floor boards. But this time, Jason, Ben and their friend decided to investigate.

The boys went outside into the dark and the last one out of the house slammed the door behind him, startling them while crashing back into the door causing Tyrone to holler.

"What happened?" he called out.

"Nothing," the boys answered all together, and Ty continued watching TV.

The boys stayed tight together as they walked toward the crawl space door. They began opening it, and heard strange sounds coming from the other side of the door. Whatever it was only stopped them from opening it momentarily. Each boy gathered up a rock or stick to protect himself and then they opened it carefully and were hit by a cold breeze blowing directly into their faces. They looked under the dark house with a flashlight to discover a huge hole under there and activity coming from it. The boys couldn't tell exactly what was going on under the house and not willing to find out. They quickly closed the crawl space door and hurried into the house and told Ty what they had discovered. Ty promised them he would check it out.

Ty then went outside to feed Cass, but instead of taking the time to confirm the boys' story, he hurried in out of the dark. He had already looked under there and didn't like what he saw the first time and had no intension of looking under the house tonight and decided to take the boys' word. It was late. Jackie would be returning home anytime now.

She came into the house smiling at Ty for the first time in days. He smiled back.

"Why are you in such a good mood?" Ty wondered.

Before she could even answer, Ty spoke again, jokingly this time. "So, Casper the Friendly Ghost lives here. Well, since he is just a little young boy spirit and it's okay with you that he's living under the house or wherever, then tell that spirit and those friends he hangs out with to keep the noise down, so I can get some sleep."

They both laughed and comforted each other.

Friday morning saw the same routine. After Jackie and the kids left, Ty decided to have a big breakfast. That was when he noticed the stove wasn't working. He went outside to check the fuse box. It had only one switch and the power was off. He turned it back on, creating a major flash, and then quickly shut it off and rushed back into the kitchen, where a surface fire burned behind the stove.

"Oh shit!"

He managed to put out the blaze but the wire protruding from the wall was still red hot. Then he heard a crackling sound.

"What the hell now?" he wondered.

The water heater was right next to the stove. Ty panicked, hopping around, feeling the floors and walls for heat while sweating profusely.

Tyrone hurried outside to see if any smoke was coming from the house. Without even thinking, he unlocked the door to the crawl space under the house and crawled in all the way to the other side. He couldn't see well and the crackling sound had him badly worried. Suddenly, Ty remembered the animal he had seen here and became instantly terrified. He kicked up so much dirt with his knees, attempting to get out of there as fast as he could that a small dust storm erupted in the enclosed space.

Tyrone was so shook up he dialed 911. Soon he could hear the fire trucks in the distance. All of the neighbors up and down the street watched as the fire engines got closer and then pulled up in front of the house.

Tyrone rushed out, covered with dirt and told the firemen what had happened.

They took a look around the house but didn't find anything burning, though they did ask a lot of questions about the wiring in the house. Tyrone gave them the name of the house's owner and told them what they wanted to know. Even though it turned out to be a false alarm, the firemen explained it was better to be safe than sorry. Again, Ty had the feeling that the house had a lot to do with his creating such a scene. What a way to end the week, he thought.

Tyrone went back inside the house and sat down, needing something to calm him down. It had been a few days since he had last tasted the pipe. He decided to call Jackie before beginning. He told her what had happened. She agreed that he probably did look crazy running and crawling around that house. She asked him to stay cool for the rest of the day and to remember to pick up Caroline from school. But Ty did better than just play it cool; he got back in touch with James.

After speaking with the firemen, Ty felt that the whole property was a fire and safety hazard. James agreed and they decided that this weekend would be a good time to cut down all the weeds and get rid of the junk around the house.

It took four guys—James, his friends Joe and Jack, along with Ty—the whole weekend to get the property back to where it could again be managed. Jackie worked the entire weekend at the restaurant, meanwhile, and Jason and Ben were gone until Sunday night while Caroline stayed at home all weekend.

On Sunday night, when the work was all done, the four men cleaned up the tools and downed a few beers.

Jackie soon pulled up into the driveway after working all day at the restaurant. She got out of the car and thanked James, Jack and Joe, then went inside the house with Caroline. She had brought food home from the restaurant. Tyrone was tired and hungry.

Joe and Jack loaded everything up and waited for James in his truck while Ty paid and thanked him again.

Ty then hurried into the house and cleaned up for dinner. Jason and Ben walked through the front door just in time, but Ben didn't eat much; he wasn't feeling well. Jackie made him wash up, gave him some medicine and sent him straight to bed.

After dinner Ty fed Cass, put Caroline into the bathtub and helped out with the dishes, as was his habit. Dishwashing time was when he and Jackie could talk to each other about the day.

"Did you run across anything else on the property this weekend?" Jackie wondered.

"As a matter of fact, yes," he replied. "There were mounds every eight feet, and once the grass was cut down, they were really noticeable. There was a large bee hive in the yard. The bees were a little bigger then usual flying in and out of it."

"Wow, it's good to know about that—I'm allergic to bee stings," she said.

"Well then, stay away from that side of the house."

Jackie got Caroline out of the bath tub and put her to bed. Ty lay down next to her and read while Jackie sat up and watched TV. She wound up falling asleep in the chair. Ty turned off the TV and put Jackie in bed with Caroline. He stretched out on the mat and fell into a deep sleep.

Chapter 7

Monday morning everyone got up except Ben, who stayed home from school, still not feeling well. Jackie left, taking Caroline and Jason to school. It was a half day of school for Caroline today. Ty made sure that Ben would be okay for the morning until Ty got back as he had to run some errands in town, after which he would go by the school and pick up Caroline.

The day went as planned and when they came home Caroline ran into the house to check on Ben who was still in bed. She wanted to make him some soup for lunch, so both Ty and Caroline ended up having soup with crackers.

Caroline wanted to be the nurse to Ben so Ty told her she could watch TV and serve as nurse for as long as she was needed.

It was a pleasant afternoon and Ty decided to have a beer. He went out onto the back steps and sat down to drink it. Around two P.M. Caroline called him to come look at her underwear. Wondering what could possibly be happening now, Ty went back inside to investigate. He discovered two pink dots moving around on the child's panties. He couldn't believe what he was seeing.

"Ben, get up," he yelled.

Ben came in to join the viewing of this extraordinary event. They all watched the pink dots moving around for several seconds before Ty told her to take off the haunted underwear. She complied quickly.

At first, Caroline wasn't frightened. She just laughed, claiming that the dots tickled. But that changed quickly when her little vagina puffed up as if was going to burst. As it continued to swell, she became acutely uncomfortable. As soon as the young girl demonstrated her fear, Ty lost it. He instinctively knew that the young spirit was going after the child. He could almost see the thing moving around inside Caroline's body. Ty's mind returned to the night of the light show. He wondered if it had used the lights to distract him while it tried to have sex with Caroline or fondled her.

Ben was just standing there in disbelief not quite with it because of all the medicine he was on.

Furious, frightened and everything in between, Ty ran a bath for the child. Once she was in the water, Ty had Ben bring a lamp. He took the shade off the lamp and brought it close to the water.

He aimed it directly at her vagina and started making crazy-sounding threats.

"I'm going to drown your ass!" He threatened the boy spirit. "Get out of her now!"

The wait was on. The water was hot. The bathroom was very small. Ty was sweating profusely. Caroline quickly gave up. She wanted out of the water and started to cry.

"Please, don't cry Caroline," Ty pleaded. "The evil spirits want you to be scared and give in."

He coached her to remain calm. Just a little longer and Tyrone believed that the spirit would be trapped and drowned in the child's body. He knew for sure it was Joseph's ghost and that young spirit could hold its breath for a long time. All of a sudden, Ty was attacked directly. Something was crawling around on him. He figured these were other spirits trying to make him drop that lamp. But he refused to let that happen. Soon he actually saw bubbles erupting from inside Caroline.

This bastard was running out of air, Ty thought, and that meant it could be destroyed.

"Die, suckers!" he muttered through clenched teeth.

He wanted to cry out. Tyrone was caught between a rock and a hard spot. He knew that if he yelled out it would scare Caroline. Pretty soon bubbles started erupting all around her. Once in a while the light would seem to get brighter. He didn't know what was making that happen, but, it was working in his favor.

Ty became so worried for Caroline that he had Ben call Jackie at work. But when the boy tried to tell Jackie what was happening, she refused to listen. Ty could tell by listening to Ben's end of the conversation that Jackie was growing angry. Sometime later, while still in the tub, Caroline glanced back and both she and Ty saw a light appear and then vanish out of the water. Then they were startled by the slam of the front door up against the wall. Ty froze and listened to the charge of feet stomping toward them. He was actually somewhat relieved once he saw that it was Jackie. With fire in her eyes she snatched Caroline out of the tub. She was mad as hell and calling Ty every crazy name in the book.

Ben came out of the room and tried to calm her down, but only made her angrier.

"You better stop brainwashing these kids," she hissed at Ty. "I am so mad with you, Ty, for putting our daughter through such nonsense, you need to be committed to a damn hospital," she screamed.

Ty's mind was working overtime. Jackie finished dressing Caroline and told her to sit down and watch TV and for Ben to go back to bed until she returned from work. Ty was glad to know that Jackie intended to go back to work as it gave him a chance to go off on that house and whoever was listening. One thing Ty knew for sure—something, or someone, was going to pay for what just had taken place.

"Nobody messes with my daughter. I am willing to die if it takes that to destroy the ghost, spirit, or whatever the hell it is in this house," he swore.

"There is no way that this young spirit is friendly!" he raged on. "There is a freaking evil spirit living here and I know how I'm going to deal with his ass!"

He started making wooden crosses as fast as he could. He put the big crosses in the shed and placed the little crosses in the house. He put them in places where Jackie would not look. He wanted to burn that young spirit and all the other spirits, along with the house, right down to the ground.

"Burn this hellhole down!" he proclaimed.

He could sense a war was on its way. Something very wrong was going to happen at this old house. He felt certain that one night the young spirit would attack everyone in the house and have his way with Jackie and Caroline. Everyone in the house was in serious danger and Ty just wanted to fight back.

"The young spirit wants to get rid of me. The young spirit wants to have life through my family. Well come on then," he challenged.

The anticipation became unbearable as nightfall grew near.

Jackie and Jason came home together. Not much was said during dinner and the two adults did not have their usual reunion party in the kitchen after dinner.

Ty fed Cass and made sure the windows and doors were all locked, then laid on the floor and stared at the TV. He was acting strangely and Jackie left him alone.

She checked in on Ben and gave him some medicine. Jason was already asleep and Caroline wasn't too far off. Jackie bent down and kissed Ty on the forehead.

"Take it easy, honey," she said.

"Good night," he responded listlessly.

Ty didn't sleep at all that night. Cass barked wildly, even crying at times. He remained awake as if he was enlisted in the army on the front lines watching for the enemy.

Believing that the evil spirit knew his daily routine Ty decided there was going to be a change in that routine. From this night on he was ready for all hell to break loose at this house.

The next day Ben stayed home again. Ty left right after Jackie, Jason and Caroline. He drove around for a while and then parked his car near Caroline's school and went to sleep.

When school let out, Caroline walked up to the car and knocked on the window to wake him up. Ty let her in and took her to get something to eat. At the restaurant, Ty found a phone booth and called Ben.

"How are you feeling?" Ty asked.

"Okay," Ben replied. "Mom called a couple of times already."

Ty promised Ben that he would see him soon. He then called Jackie to let her know where he and Caroline were and that when they finished, they would head back to the house.

Jackie told Ty that Carla and John wanted go out to dinner tonight and had invited them along.

"I'll see how I feel after I get home." he replied and hung up. Ty couldn't stand John, and didn't want to go to dinner with him. In any case, he had plans for that house and was not going anywhere else.

Carla and John showed up at the old house on Newton Street the same time Jackie and Jason did.

"Are you going to come to dinner with us?" Jackie wanted to know.

"No," Ty answered, knowing he couldn't leave the house, he couldn't even explain that they were all in a life or death situation. He had to stay home and try to burn, kill every unwanted presence there with the crosses he had made and hidden away earlier. Instead, he told them he was not feeling well. He thanked Carla and John for their offer. He told Ben to try eating something. "Have a good time. I will see everyone later," he said. Hopefully, he added to himself. Ty watched as Jackie and the kids left with them.

After everyone left for dinner, Ty knew he would have to rely on what he trusted and believed in. He was ready to set the house on fire. He couldn't wait to set the house on fire!

He went out to the shed and got the large crosses and brought them into the house and aimed them towards the place where he suspected the unwanted creatures originated and he would be praying for the crosses to burn them. Soon the rumbling sounds started emanating from the walls. The noises were followed by the sound of flames. Ty could feel the heat. The hotter it became the more intense it got. Ty responded in a rage.

"Come on, you mother!"

The more noise the house made, the more he went off.

"Let's get it on! Come on, you lowlifes!"

His challenge brought out all the unwanted spirits from every corner of the house. Ty held out a flaming cross. He was aiming for the cat-like eyes he saw floating everywhere. He set fire to them, stabbing into the darkness.

Ty stood in a burning house. Even though he couldn't see the flames he could feel and hear them and smell them consuming the house.

"I knew it! You are a bunch of sorry creatures! Welcome to my friendly party and die." he said.

The spirits were on Ty, all over him. He would put the crosses on himself and felt the spirits burn as they tried to penetrate his body. It was dramatic! Absurd! And unreal! But it was real as real could get. It was a major war; Ty didn't know how long this was going to continue. He was preparing to go all night if he had to. He had no choice.

Even though the house was engulfed in flames, the disembodied spirits seemed to be on a mission and just kept on coming full force. Ty's nerves were gone and the sweat was dripping off his body from the spectral heat. The old house was blazing out of control. Or so it seemed.

Ty was standing right in the middle of the inferno, making the unwanted hell rise from underneath the house. He felt good! He believed his method was working. The Higher Power was on his side. Still, he was unsure as to how this was going to end.

Next thing he heard was a car pulling up, followed by Jackie saying good-bye to Carla and John. He then heard their car start up and drive away.

Ty was standing in the middle of the living room, a cross in each of his hands. As they approached, Ty began racing through the house putting things back in place before Jackie, Jason, Ben and Caroline strolled into this mess, Jackie entered carrying Caroline and caught Ty with some things not yet put away.

He expected Jason and Ben to follow right behind her, but they had gone with Carla and John to spend the night at their house. For that, Ty was grateful. His eyes were all bugged out and sweat rolled down his forehead. He was sober and tired, every bit of life drained out of him.

Jackie began yelling, as always, saying she wanted Ty out of the house. He knew better, he wasn't going anywhere. She was angry about the mess he had made of the house right after they all left for dinner.

"I'll get it all put away," he promised weakly.

"Right now, with all the crosses and crap," she demanded.

Jackie continued going off as she laid Caroline down in the boys' room.

As he scrambled to put the rest of the cushions from the couch and other things away, Caroline woke up from all Jackie's yelling. Ty became even more stressed, worrying about Caroline seeing him in this state of mind. He knew it was scary for her. Being seven years old and under a lot of stress was dangerous. He knew changes had to be made. But this was the only place they could stay for now and it was war here. Not for long, he hoped. But for now, he had no choice but to stay and keep fighting.

That night things got worse, just as Ty anticipated. Fortunately, he had plenty of small crosses hidden in the house—in the closets and in the drawers. He refused to leave as Jackie demanded but she made it very hard for him in his war with the spirits. She wanted all the lights in the house turned off. Without the lights on, Ty felt he was a dead man. The crosses and the lights were his strongest defense, he believed. He knew for a fact that the crosses were working.

They fought back and forth. He would turn on the lights and she would shut them off.

"Please, listen to what I have to say," he begged.

Jackie did not want to hear it.

"Get out of my house!" she demanded repeatedly.

Ty was convinced that the young evil spirit had Jackie fooled. It seemed to him that she was on the spirit's side without even knowing it. Little did she know, or even realize, that the house was still on supernatural fire. Believe it, this house was on fucking fire! It wasn't visible for the eyes to see, but Ty could sense the fire still burning.

Jackie simply would not—or could not—see or feel what Ty was experiencing at that moment. Why she didn't, he could not understand—especially after what she had clearly experienced and seen for herself in this house. He was frightened for her and Caroline and was overwhelmed with fright for himself. He knew the evil spirits were mocking and laughing at him; they even had control over Jackie and there was nothing he could do, no matter how desperately he tried. The spirits kept getting stronger. It was the young spirit's house and Ty was convinced that the boy had an infinite number of followers, lost souls who had somehow followed him to this place, where Ty was the unwanted guest—and knew it.

The next time Jackie turned off the light. Tyrone stood in the middle of the front room in the pitch dark, watching a very large and powerful black panther with glowing yellow eyes—the same eyes he had seen under the house—crawling toward him. He felt a tightening in his chest and could barely breathe.

"Fuck this!" he said.

He tried to knock Jackie down out of the way. She was not only keeping her hand over the light switch in the front room but she was also standing directly in the path to the front door.

He flicked the light switch and grabbed Caroline right off the couch without any shoes or jacket and they ran outside, where Ty snatched up a cross and the pair ran into the car. Ty sat inside the car with the dome light on and the engine running, trying to figure out what to do next or where to go.

Jackie came to the front door and stood there. She looked disfigured, as if she had been transformed into something very old, sad and confused.

"Dad, mom looks scary," Caroline said and she did.

Ty was indifferent by this point. He felt empty; he had escaped the house for the time being. Jackie just stared at the car and then started to cry. This hurt Ty badly. He knew she was being used and was going to continue to be used by the things in the house, and there would be nothing he could do about it.

He rolled down the window.

Jackie spoke. "You can have the lights on. Please come back inside."

Ty knew then that she had become aware of something. She felt something. Even though she wasn't herself, and had been overcome by something in the house, he felt he could sense her true feelings. She was very frightened. From his perspective, he and Caroline didn't have anywhere else to go. And if he drove in his current state, he would be pulled over by the police and taken straight to jail. That would have been right where that young spirit would want him. Or, better yet, he would wind up in an insane asylum where nobody would believe a word he said. Ty believed the boy, Joseph, wanted him out of the way so he could persuade his family to join him in that house for as long as he needed them.

Ty told himself over and over again that he could not let that happen. He felt responsible for what was happening to his family and hated it. But he still had to deal with it.

He kept that in mind as well. There was only one path for him and that was the Higher Power's way and Ty knew he needed to straighten up.

"I've got to go back into that house and survive." he told himself.

Ty turned off the car and got out, carrying Caroline nervously in one arm, with a cross in the other, headed back toward the door. He was looking at Jackie, telling Cass to be quiet; she had been barking all night.

Ty felt himself beginning to take control as soon as he crossed the threshold. He pulled out the bed and told Jackie and Caroline to try and get some sleep. They were tired and it was late. Caroline fell fast asleep, but Ty remained uncertain about Jackie. Her eyes were closed, but was she sleeping? Ty just hoped and prayed that he could remain awake.

He placed a couple of large crosses over the covers on the girls' in the bed. He put crosses all along the bed and sat down holding one, pointing it toward them.

The spectral fire was still burning in all the corners, in the dark areas of the house.

The bed was ablaze with the supernatural fire while they occupied it, seemingly unharmed. Ty did not want anything to enter their bodies and take their souls. It was difficult staying up all night. Had he not made all those crosses and put them in the right places, he believed his family would not have survived the night.

By the crack of dawn the fires were out. The smoke had cleared and the house seemed to have settled. Ty rose unsteadily out of the chair and went around the house gathering up all of the visible crosses.

He put them back in the shed and fed Cass. He came back trying very hard not to make a sound as he didn't want to wake up the girls. By the time they got up he had already cleaned himself up and was trying hard to erase any memories from the previous night.

Ty did not know what to expect from Jackie that morning. He came into the bathroom while she was getting dressed and offered to take her to work and Caroline to school.

"Okay," she agreed.

"Would you like to go to lunch with me today?" he asked.

"I would like that," Jackie said, and smiled.

Odd, thought Ty. It was as if she didn't remember what happened the night before.

The morning had gone well as they locked up the house and left. Ty pulled into the parking lot at Jackie's work with a few minutes to spare. She asked him what plans he had made for the day. Without answering, he kissed her as she left the car.

"I'll be on time," he promised.

As he drove away, Caroline gave him a girly smile. She had been smiling the whole ride from the time they left the house.

"Mom and Dad are going to lunch," Caroline announced happily.

Ty got hugs and kisses from her as she was getting out of the car at school. She told him to have a nice lunch with Mom and went racing toward the line of kids headed into her classroom. Ty hung out getting in the last wave as the door closed behind her.

He pulled away from the school in a hurry, glancing up at the speed limit and looking into the rear view mirror. He wanted to make it to his brother-in-law's Steve's house. Steve usually left early in the mornings and was a difficult man to catch up with during the day. Ty was hoping that his sister Rene would not be around because he wanted to talk to Steve alone.

He was in luck; Rene's car was gone and Steve was in the garage. Ty parked his car across the street.

As he walked toward the garage, Steve turned around and saw him.

"Hey, what going on?" Steve asked.

"Not a whole lot," Ty replied. "Where's the lady of the house?"

"Rene left for work a few minutes ago," he answered.

Ty began beating around the bush but Steve had a pretty good guess at what Ty had come to talk about.

"Ty, if you want to come to work with me or just hang around until it's time to pick up Caroline from school every day, you're more than welcome," Steve said.

"Thanks. That helps. Maybe I will start with you next Monday. I can at least involve myself with something positive during the day, instead of feeling trapped in that house. That Newton place has really given me the creeps, not to mention causing me to have problems with Jackie."

"Well, try not to let that old house get the best of you, and let me know what your plans are. Give me a call," Steve smiled boosting Ty's spirits.

"For sure, thanks, I will call you," Ty answered as they both prepared to leave.

Ty drove back to Jackie's work and hung out in the parking lot until lunch time. Then he and Jackie had lunch at the restaurant where she worked nights. They talked and laughed and had a good time. It had been a while since the two of them had lunched together. He asked her if she had heard from Jason and Ben. Jackie responded that they were going to spend the rest of the week at Carla's house.

"Well, looks like we will almost have the house to ourselves," Ty said, almost forgetting their other guests.

Jackie smiled, and replied, "I won't be working too late tonight."

On the drive back to work, Ty told Jackie he had decided to start working with Steve the following Monday.

"That's a good idea," she agreed.

Ty let her out of the car and promised that he and Caroline would be on time picking her up from work. He kissed her and said good-bye and headed on over to Caroline's school.

By the time he got there she was coming out of class.

She came to the car and before she even said hello, wanted to know about lunch.

"How was lunch with Mom?"

"Lunch was good, and how was your day in school?" he asked.

"I had a good day too," Caroline answered.

"How would you like to go to McDonald's?" he asked.

Caroline cheered, "McDonald's!"

They sang the McDonald's song all the way and spent the entire day there. After Caroline ate, she did all her homework on the spot. Then Ty let her play in the McDonald's playground.

When the time came to pick up Jackie, he called to Caroline, and off they went.

On the way to Jackie's work Ty did a lot of thinking. The idea of going back to the old house after sunset bothered him. Ty thought that giving the spirits the house all to themselves as much as possible could perhaps work in his favor. Still that would be something he would have to put to the test.

Jackie and a few of the other ladies were walking out into the parking lot just as Ty and Caroline showed up. Jackie got into the car and greeted Caroline. Ty interrupted briefly.

"Did the boss let everyone off a little early?" he asked.

Jackie smiled and said, "The day couldn't have gone any better."

Then Caroline burst out telling her mother about her McDonald's adventure. In the meantime, Ty was still thinking about the darkness on the horizon. Jackie had plenty of time before she had to be at the restaurant, so Ty asked her if they could be dropped off at the house first.

Jackie agreed, and they made it back to the house before it got dark. Jackie dropped them off and promised Ty that she would call a little later. As Caroline and Ty went inside, he felt a little bit better.

Ty got Caroline cleaned up and fed Cass. They had dinner and then he got himself a bath while Caroline watched TV. She was fast asleep by the time he finished cleaning up. Ty sat down afterwards and watched TV and listened to the noise under the house.

A few hours later, the phone rang, startling him. It was Jackie letting him know that she was off work and had a little surprise: he already knew what the surprise was going to be, but told her to be careful and hurry home.

Ty sat still waiting and listening for Jackie's car to pull up in the driveway. When she finally arrived, he was waiting on the porch.

Jackie got out of the car and smiled. "Does my man miss me?"

Tyrone laughed and replied, "Get in here, woman!"

She handed him a bottle of wine. "Is Caroline asleep?" she whispered.

"Yes, she's been out like a light for a while."

Jackie went straight into the bathroom and got cleaned up while Ty poured the wine.

She returned from the bathroom and he was waiting for her in the boys' room with a candle lit and the window cracked open.

They started smoking, drinking and making out. Everything was fine until a powerfully disturbing sensation overcame Ty. He felt the house was about to react in a violent way.

"What's wrong? Are you all right?" she asked.

"No! We better leave the house—right away," Tyrone said.

"For how long?"

"I don't know." Ty didn't know the length of time, but he did know he was not going to be second guessing his feelings; and his feelings just knew it was time to leave.

Jackie didn't ask any more questions as she dressed and wrapped a blanket around Caroline. Tyrone quickly locked the window, threw on clothes and grabbed a couple of wooden crosses.

They left in Jackie's car and it was cold outside. Poor Caroline didn't know what was going on as she was laid on the back seat of the car not saying a word.

As Tyrone drove down the street, they heard noises— pouncing, banging—coming from the trunk. Ty pulled the car over and got out, clutching one of the crosses, and opened the trunk enough to throw in the cross and slam it closed. There was a sharp crack he could only assume was the cross bursting into flames, followed by a scratching and scrambling as if something was trying to escape the trunk.

Ty leapt back in the car and drove about a half mile down Del Monte Blvd., when they heard a bang. Jackie, looking at the side view mirror, said, "The trunk looks like it's open!"

Tyrone confirmed that the trunk was open. He looked at Jackie, puzzled. "I closed that trunk down tight." He stopped the car, got out, and looked in the trunk. It was empty, so closed it again.

Back on the road, they decided to stop at Kevin's house. Ty wasn't ready to go back to the house on Newton Street. Ty tried to explain to his friend what had been happening, but it was no use. Kevin was up to nothing but no good, just like they were.

Kevin didn't believe a word Tyrone uttered but that didn't surprise him, as he suspected Kevin's sole motive was to get next to Jackie. Kevin didn't disappoint him, telling Jackie that he wanted to drop Tyrone off at the hospital because Tyrone was crazy. Tyrone knew that this rationale was designed so Kevin could get Jackie high and try to do her.

"I'm not going to no hospital, so you can get that out of your mind right now," Ty told Kevin. Ty and Jackie passed a couple of hours at Kevin's house in the bathroom getting high and screwing on the bathroom floor. Caroline remained asleep all along, thankfully. When Ty and Jackie came out of the bathroom. Ty asked Kevin and Jackie to go back to the house on Newton Street with him while a friend of Kevin's watched over Caroline.

When they returned to the old house, the trio sat on the sofa and talked about nothing; at least nothing Tyrone wanted to hear—especially from Kevin. Ty was trying to sense whether the house was safe enough to bring Caroline back as it was now around two A.M. He decided to wait until the sun came up before bringing Caroline back to old house on Newton Street.

Before leaving, Ty placed his golf clubs all over the floor, making crosses out of them. The house reacted to that, and he knew the spirits were going to reappear. The situation was climaxing when they left. The sounds of thunder rumbling throughout the house.

When they returned to Kevin's, Jackie and Tyrone started a crack smoking binge. They smoked in his house and Ty began to realize Kevin's place was not safe either; everywhere the family fled, the evil spirits would follow. The spirits wouldn't stop until their mission was completed. And it was obvious that the longer they stayed in the old house, the more of an uphill battle they would face. The spirits were trying to destroy and kill them. Tyrone really wanted things to be different, but did not have a choice in the matter. Tyrone was ready for more confrontations and more fighting.

Evil and destruction were at hand. Deterioration of some minds and spirits was upon them and in time, souls would be taken.

Chapter 8

The sun came up and everyone was still partying. When Tyrone and Jackie finally left Kevin's and returned to the old house, the fun and games continued. It had been a long night for Caroline, who had been moved all around but she fell back to sleep once Jackie laid her into bed.

The adults went into the kitchen and immediately started smoking and having sex. As she took a hit, he bent her over holding onto the sink. When he took a hit, she sucked him so well he would stand on his toes gasping for that last breath of air while he held in the smoke. They were having a nasty old time.

Suddenly, Tyrone felt as if they were being watched. Someone or something was at the back door. Ty started talking dirty loudly enough for whomever or whatever it was to hear them. The breathing of something awful, large and tall was clearly audible outside the door. But they were enjoying the sex and getting too high to stop and really check it out.

However, the sound was building enough on the other side of the door to induce Ty to stop indulging in Jackie's hot womb for a short period. But he had no intention of opening the door. He tried to determine whether it was an animal or person. There was an opening at the top of the door. He tried peeking out of the opening but had no luck seeing anything as it was very dark outside. He decided to put a piece of meat at the top of the door to see if the being was a large animal and would eat the meat. He determined it wasn't an animal because it didn't touch the meat. Nonetheless, Ty felt that the nature of the entity didn't make a difference as it would have to kick the door down to stop them from partying.

All of a sudden, Jackie let out a cry and her watch fell off her wrist and onto the floor. She collapsed and he caught her.

"Damn! What happened, baby?" Ty asked, shaking her. He held her and they stared at each other. She had no memory of what had just occurred. Tyrone had become silent when tears started falling; every sound that came from his throat trembled.

Jackie voiced one request: "Please don't say anything to Jason and Ben about this."

It was a sign of awareness for her. As Ty saw it, death was right around the corner. It didn't seem to matter that they were on a runaway train. She recovered and he bent her back over and they continued doing the nasty until they ran out of dope, at which point Tyrone left to score more.

Thursday and all through the night, was awfully tough. Jackie called into work sick and Caroline missed school, having to practically take care of herself.

The adults kept drinking, smoking, and screwing. Jackie managed to doze off every now and then. Tyrone couldn't sleep; Cass' barking and howling on top of all the other strange noises and movements in the house were too much for him.

Friday morning he went out to check on Cass, and noticed a change in her immediately. When he came in from feeding her, he mentioned to Jackie that Cass wouldn't come to him; Cass had just looked at him like she had never seen her master before. Jackie said it was because Ty looked so bad. Tyrone didn't respond. He was deep in thought and she was so freaking out of it. He was trying to anticipate the young spirit's next move and believed Cass had had a bad experience—perhaps with that animal they had seen under the house. Ty decided there was no way that young Joseph or that animal was going to get at him through his damn dog!

Tyrone shook Jackie who had dozed off and told her he wanted to have Cass checked out at the animal hospital. Jackie looked up.

"There is nothing wrong with that damn dog. Please lie down and try to get some rest."

Tyrone's mind raced. As he paced the floor, he picked up the phone and made a couple of phone calls, including one to Cass's veterinarian. He told the vet that he moved and Cass was no longer in a fenced yard and could get pregnant as soon as she came in heat. Could she get fixed right away?

The veterinarian had an opening for 1:00 that afternoon. Although Ty knew he couldn't take her to the hospital in the shape he was in, he accepted the appointment anyway.

The next call was to Ty's youngest brother, Eric, who wasn't home. His wife Stacy answered and said she would be happy to take Cass to the hospital. Eric and Stacy owned one of Cass' litter mates, and Stacy thought it was an excellent idea to have Cass spayed.

Stacy told him that she would be over shortly. After hanging up the phone all Ty had to do was get cleaned up before she arrived. He could at least change the clothes he had been wearing for the past couple of days.

When Stacy showed up, Cass jumped into her car. Ty gave Stacy the money for the operation and asked her to keep him informed on any details. She said she would call him as soon as the operation was over and let him know when Cass could come home.

He went back inside the house where Jackie still slept. Caroline was up and wanted to know where Cass was going.

"Cass is going to the animal hospital to get a check up," Ty explained.

"What kind of a check up?" Caroline asked with concern.

"A kind of check up vets give to animals to make sure they're healthy," Ty explained.

"Is Cass going to have babies?" she asked.

Ty knew then that Caroline had been listening to his conversation with the vet and with Stacy.

"No, Cass is not going to have puppies. As a matter of fact the vet is going to make sure that Cass doesn't get pregnant," said Ty.

"How come Cass can't have puppies? I would like for her to have puppies one day."

"Caroline, we don't have the place for puppies. I'm sorry." Ty ended the conversation and three hours later the phone rang. It was Stacy calling about Cass. She would not be released until Monday afternoon. Stacy said that the veterinarian had explained that Cass had a highly enlarged and abnormal uterus. It was shocking but Tyrone was not surprised; he knew all along something strange had taken place with Cass. He thanked her one more time and hung up.

He let Caroline know Cass would be home Monday afternoon and everything was okay. He sat back and rationalized that at least he was making it hard for the spirits.

Jackie finally got back up after sleeping all day and fed Caroline and ate something herself. Tyrone was feeling victorious, and went into the boys' room and started smoking again.

Late that night the bottom fell out on Tyrone. Jackie joined him in the boys' room after Caroline went to sleep and began feeling as good as Tyrone already did. Jackie got comfortable and just laid next to Tyrone.

He started rubbing her body. Everything was fine until Ty noticed that she was overreacting to the simple caressing. He then realized that he had company. The young boy spirit had joined him and Jackie in bed. At first he was startled and then a bit frightened, the young spirit had already made his move on Jackie. Ty knew it and suddenly it became a race to see who was going to get into Jackie's vagina first. Tyrone had a disadvantage: Jackie still had her pants on. However, her possession by the boy spirit would take place even if her pants were on. Joseph got her before Ty did; he had help in distracting Tyrone from all directions; under the sheets, the bed shook and the windows rattled. Ty had to get her pants off if he was going to have a chance.

While they were in bed, he also had to keep an eye on Caroline who was in the living room. Tyrone was confused for a minute and did not know which way to turn. His biggest concern was Caroline, as Jackie had already been had. Tyrone didn't think he had a chance, but he quickly got up from Jackie, went into the living room, and put a cross on Caroline so the cross would burn any seed that evil spirit tried to plant.

Joseph had claimed Jackie's vagina as his. He wanted it to himself but Tyrone was still going to fight back, so he got back into bed with Jackie and Joseph.

What happened next blew Tyrone's mind—and his wad. He was determined to get an erection. When he did, he started trying to put it inside Jackie, but Joseph blocked him from the inside. Ty used his fingers and as soon as he did Joseph opened her vagina so wide Ty's whole hand went in. Damn! He was amazed. Another trick, but as unbelievable as it may sound, he got turned on.

Tyrone spoke out, "What in the hell is happening here?" Jackie's vagina was not only huge but very, very hot. He exploded, collapsed, melted, and shrunk all at the same time. He was being drained of his erection.

"This is crazy! This evil spirit is sucking me off," he said to himself. That was what it felt like as his orgasms went on and on. He tried stopping it.

"Enough already," he ordered.

He knew something was wrong; it felt good but scary. He tried to move up and down but the heat and sensation were too much. Tyrone was being sucked alive by a giant vagina. What a night this was turning out to be.

"What am I going to do?" he asked out loud. He didn't know. He sat up naked in the bed, scared stiff.

Tyrone climbed out of bed and peeked into the room where Caroline was. Yellow eyes peered out underneath the couch between the cushions; Tyrone's heart was pumping.

He looked back toward the bed, and Jackie was still lying there. He tried to get her attention but she was out in another zone. The spirits swarmed over and around her like a bunch of buzzards pecking away at her flesh.

Tyrone reached down on the floor and picked up a large cross, along with the sweatpants he had been wearing. He put his pants on and leaned the cross up against the wall, aiming it towards Jackie. Then Tyrone prayed to the Higher Power to spare her soul. That was all she had left. He left a dim light on in the dining room so he could see what he was doing. He gathered more crosses, and put them all around Caroline, and then lay down next to her in defeat.

When the sun rose, Tyrone put the big crosses away and tried to get some rest. This weekend was not over by far, and there was a lot left to smoke.

Saturday was no different from Friday, except that the young spirit and Ty were both well aware of the other. Ty knew one of them had the upper hand on Jackie; he also knew it wasn't him.

For the second time, Jackie had been raped. Tyrone felt the room closing in, and heard the sound effects of her vagina as the young spirit continued to indulge in it. Tyrone frustratingly found himself aroused by the sounds of sex.

Ty listened and watched while the young spirit and several other evil spirits fought in having their share of Jackie. They were a bunch of out of control animals. She was moaning, groaning, smiling, and moving her lips and mouth. It had come down to an actual fight with this young spirit over her vagina. It became difficult for Tyrone to have sex with her.

When he tried, they came from everywhere. He would turn and see them emerging from the bottom of the bed covers and he would kick at them. He looked under the covers and saw the soaked sheets. Jackie's pubic hair was covered with semen, and there were bruises down the insides of her legs. She bruised easily anyway for as long as he had known her.

This whole thing was out of hand and wrong. The evil spirit had engaged in a full sexual relationship with Jackie; she was in deep trouble, but Ty could only watch helplessly, devoted to her as he was.

He hurt for Jackie, for all of them; he wanted to scream, he needed help so badly, but he was just frozen, watching.

This evil spirit had control of Jackie's body and mind and it was too late; it had had its way with her. The lowest spirit of all had invaded his life. Jackie was being humped and humped and it seemed she was loving every minute of her new relationship.

It angered Ty and filled him with all kinds of mixed-up feelings; his self-control was in question, and he hated it. He started crying as he died inside.

Everything around him began to feel frightening. The dope was all gone now and his mindset started changing and gearing up for trouble. The blame for this rode heavily on his shoulders. He fell for it all the way but decided he was not going to give up. He knew the bottom line: he had to stay alive and awaken to watch over Caroline the rest of the night, and he did just that.

Jackie got up Sunday afternoon happy and in a hurry. She missed church but she and Caroline were going to meet up with her mother for lunch before Jackie had to be at work. She was a functioning addict, Ty noted, as she and Caroline left the house and drove away. He wondered what she could possibly be so happy about.

When he arrived at Jackie's workplace to pick up Caroline, Ty noticed a difference in Jackie. She was still jolly but showed very little attention toward him.

"Is everything all right?" he asked her.

She just toyed with him a bit, and mentioned that it would be nice to wake up every morning to the dream that she'd had this morning.

"It was that good you say?" he asked with a sly smile.

"Don't even try and flatter yourself," she replied. She just recalled how good it was, but could not tell him with whom she had been.

She had to get back to work so she said good-bye to Caroline and told Ty he looked awful and should go back to the house and try to get some rest.

Caroline and Ty drove back to the house. His mind was going a thousand miles a second just thinking back on everything. Jackie thought everything happening to her at the house was just a dream! That's all he needed, for her to be enjoying it all.

Ty was glad to see that Jason and Ben were at the house when they arrived. They had been fishing and decided to have fish for dinner. Caroline went into the kitchen to watch them prepare it.

Ty turned on the TV and lay down on the couch, slept all through dinner, and woke up around nine P.M.

Jackie walked into the house in the same mood she'd been in when she had left the house that morning. She spent a little time with the kids and then everyone prepared for bed. Ty was feeling a little left out but did not bring anything up in what little conversation they had that night.

He waited to make sure everyone was asleep, and then brought out a couple of crosses and placed them around Jackie and Caroline. He also kept the TV and kitchen light on all night.

Tyrone lay down on the floor and keyed in on the same old sounds coming from the house that he had been listening to for weeks. He was exhausted and made one last check on Caroline and the boys to make sure they were fine. He got himself a cross and lay back down. He started repeating the Lord's Prayer over and over until he could not hear himself anymore.

Caroline was the first up in the morning. Luckily Tyrone was sleeping right next to her on the floor. She practically stepped on him as she climbed out of the sofa bed. Ty's eyes opened, and he quickly arose to remove the crosses before Jackie saw them. His thoughts about what could have taken place with her throughout the night while he was sleeping came to mind, but once she and the kids were up and going, all talking at the same time over breakfast, it didn't matter anymore; everyone in the house was alive.

Ty got a perfunctory good morning greeting from Jackie, but nothing more. He decided to accept this little change in her for now as he didn't know what else to do.

He told the kids he was taking them to school; Ben and Jason went outside and waited in Ty's car. Caroline and Jackie finished getting ready while Ty phoned Steve, to tell him Cass had to be picked up from the hospital that morning and he would start work tomorrow morning instead.

Caroline helped Ty lock up and they walked Jackie out to her car. Ty promised he would call her later; they all said good-bye and Ty and Caroline hurried back to his car.

He followed Jackie until she reached her turn off, and then continued on straight, taking the boys to school first. Caroline did not want to go to school; she wanted to pick up Cass, but Ty promised her Cass would be in the car when he returned for her after school. He dropped her off and headed to the valley, where he spent just enough time at the vet to pay and get instructions on when to change Cass's bandages. He still wasn't in the best of shape and did not want anyone to catch on to how nervous he felt at times.

Cass was certainly glad to see him and anxious to leave the hospital; she wouldn't sit still in the car for several miles down the road. Since Ty still had three more hours before it was time to pick up Caroline, he drove to the beach and parked the car. Cass was in no shape to go for a walk so they just sat back in the seat and watched the waves.

When Ty arrived to pick up Caroline, she was so excited to see Cass. On the way home Tyrone explained Cass's condition to her, explaining that she would have to help Cass relax inside the house. Jackie did not care for animals in the house at all, but Cass could not stay outdoors with an open wound.

As soon as Cass got inside the house, Ty knew she sensed something wrong. She started sniffing around and began acting strangely. She would appear to chase something throughout the house that none of them could see. She started jumping up on the window sills and sometimes tried to dig through the floors.

Tyrone just sat down for a while, watching. He believed she had that young spirit running from corner to corner to corner, trying to hide or get away. He would say "Get him, Cass," and she would just go crazy and run him out of the house.

Ty finally calmed his dog down and put her in the room by the front door, and closed the door that led to the living room where they slept at night.

After all the excitement, Ty went into the kitchen and fixed Caroline something to eat. While she ate, he swept up the dog hair throughout the house. Caroline wanted to be the one checking on Cass and Ty agreed because he knew she would be safe around Cass.

After Ty helped Caroline with her homework, he called Jackie to see where her mind was at. He briefly told her about Cass being home and that she would be okay. He explained that Cass would stay in the room by the front door.

"That's okay with me," she said.

He then asked her if she had to work that night.

"No."

"Well, I'll see you when you get home," he told her.

That was the end of the conversation.

Tyrone hung up the phone and got angry; he could feel the tension building and resented being treated like an outsider.

During the next four days things continued to get worse. In the mornings the air in the house grew thinner, and it was becoming obviously colder. Each time he took a breath and then exhaled or even spoke, smoke would pour from Ty's mouth like a dragon spewing fire.

Jackie and Tyrone communicated very little with each other. He would hurry to leave the house as he hated seeing her fall more and more under the influence of whatever haunted this place. He took the kids to school since it was on the way to Steve's house.

Each afternoon after picking up Caroline from school, Cass was allowed to chase the spirits throughout the house. She wouldn't let anything settle down until Jackie came home from work at night. Ty had been dealing with the kids all week as well as working and reliving each night by relating every little detail of what happened in the house to Steve.

By late Friday night Ty lay on the sofa bed, worn out mentally and physically. He was feeling weak all of a sudden, as if he were tripping, only not on drugs, just tripping. Jackie and the kids were asleep.

Cass started moving around and looking out her door to see what ever she could. Ty was trying to relax but his sides hurt. It was more than just Cass's recovery worrying him, or the sex those evil spirits were having with Jackie, or even the noise and movement throughout the house. It was the way he was feeling. What was happening to him? Ty felt for his testicles and they were practically gone. He could smash them and it didn't even hurt; he was being robbed and felt like he was being poisoned, being operated on in the groin. The spirits had gotten to him while he was dazed. Then the rumbling started throughout the walls and floors; shadows started appearing around corners.

Tyrone got up and turned the porch light on and set the dining room light on dim. It gave him enough light so that he would have a chance to see anything coming toward him. He then put a cross over Caroline and one over Jackie. Cass couldn't go through the house the way Ty would have liked; it was too late at night and Jackie would wake up and go crazy. He also didn't want Jackie turning the lights out.

Suddenly, the room and bed lit up in spectral flames. Ty didn't quite understand the evil spirit's intolerance of fire since Hell was one big pit of fire. Anyway, the spirits were being burned by the crosses, but the entities kept coming. Ty tried to sit in a chair with his back up against the window, but it was just too nerve-wracking. He had to get away from the window, but first he looked out into the front yard and saw a casket with his name inscribed on it. That explained all the noises and knocking sounds coming from under the house; they had been making a casket.

Tyrone wasn't dreaming; he was wide awake and could not believe what was taking place. He eased his way back to the bed. He couldn't wait to get under the cover as he expected to be attacked in full force. He was trying to prepare but he wished and hoped for help. He started chanting and praying softly, saying the Lord's Prayer over and over, and talking about how much he believed in the Higher Power and that the Higher Power was on the way to help him. Tyrone talked compulsively, believing every word that came out of his mouth, because that was why he'd made it this far. The pressure was on; he looked at Jackie and she was asleep.

Tyrone got up to put Cass on a chain and walked her around inside the house. If Jackie woke up, he would tell her he was taking Cass out for a walk.

When he finally returned to bed, Ty tried to pull the covers over his head, but couldn't as when he tried to scoot down into the bed, his feet hung out. Besides, if the covers were over his head, how would he keep the crosses on Jackie and Caroline? He knew that wouldn't work; the only thing he could do was to just lie there, terrified.

The next morning was the start of the weekend and the days passed quickly. Ty was anticipating another all-nighter, watching and waiting for that big, black, yellow-eyed creature to appear in front of them and leap on him. The only questions were how many at once and how big were they going to be?

Once again, Ty spent a stressful night trying to stay alive, counting the hours until sunrise, living a nightmare.

Everything he saw and heard was so plain and clear. He really had to work on keeping his breathing under control, so his heart wouldn't beat so loudly. Ty could not let those spirits know he was scared—very scared. It would just give them more strength.

He lay there with his eyes bugged out. They either became so dry they hurt from staring or else they ran like a faucet and burned. His mouth hung open and saliva built up and poured down the corner of his mouth and dripped onto his arm. He didn't even notice it until he would almost choke to death swallowing a mouthful all at once. Everything seemed to be working in the young spirit's favor. It was all about Ty staying alive and awake, no matter what.

Ty felt he was getting closer and closer to death each night at this house with every encounter. His nerves gone and his energy drained, he was at the end of the road. He'd been up all night as usual, but was sober and straight with nothing but horror running through his veins. Tyrone had no idea that this would be his last weekend at this haunted house.

The sun finally came up, shining through the windows. Suddenly his attention was drawn toward the chest under the dining room windows. It was slowly opening! Ty jumped out of bed and rushed over to hold it down; something was trying to force its way out. He then hurried to the drawer where he kept a hammer and some nails, raced back, and hammered the nails into the chest as fast as he could. Something was pushing the nails out as quickly as Ty could pound them in. He panicked and rushed into the boys' room to get Ben out of bed. Half asleep the boy stumbled back with Ty to stand by the chest.

"Do you see this?" Tyrone asked him. While the boy didn't answer, Ty continued hammering frantically, until it was finally nailed down. When he turned to ask Ben for help, he saw the boy had already left the room and gone back to bed. Without hesitation, Ty cried aloud for help as if with his last breath. Right away the distraction in the chest stopped as if nothing happened. Jackie woke up, furious, and Caroline lay puzzled, scared and quiet, but Ty didn't care. He couldn't understand why it took Jackie so long to wake up in the first place, considering all the noise he'd been making.

Chapter 9

Tyrone moved quickly, trying to remove all of the crosses within Jackie's sight but he was too late. She was out of control, screaming at him to get all of the crosses out of the house.

It was terrible how she had changed overnight once again. She did not look like herself. She seemed old, drained, pale, heavily bruised, and out of breath. If Tyrone had to describe her demeanor, he would swear she was possessed. Tyrone knew then that the young spirit had penetrated deep into her soul, and was acting through her.

He tried explaining to her how important it was to stick together and to leave this house for good. He resolved that no matter what she decided, he and Caroline were moving. Where he didn't care at this point.

He was praying and crying to the Higher Power. "I hoped that one day I could make it all right, but, this is it!" Tyrone yelled. He continued calling for answers, he wanted answers to all the questions on his mind. In desperation he blurted: "Let's call a psychic hotline!"

"What? Not from this house!" Jackie hissed.

Tyrone pleaded. "Come on! If you won't let me do it for us, then let me make a call for Caroline's sake." It was no use; Jackie would not support him at all.

Nonetheless, Tyrone took a deep breath and continued with the plans that were already forming in his mind.

He was putting it all in the Higher Power's hands; Tyrone was going to follow his beliefs.

Ty grabbed the Yellow Pages, and then headed for the phone. He called information, asking for the local psychic hotline listings. There were none.

"I am not looking for a palm reading," he told the operator.

He hung up, trying to gather his thoughts in order to try again. This time he asked for a long distance number toll free or not and a number came up, out in New Jersey. He wrote it down, and then dialed the number. A woman answered. He barely gave her a chance to say hello.

He stuttered, "I...I have a problem, can you help me?" In fifteen seconds, he explained he lived in Monterey with Caroline, Ben, Jason and his girlfriend, Jackie, in a haunted house. "There are bad things happening here at this house," he said.

There was a short pause.

"Give me your name and race," she asked.

He told her his name, and that he was black.

"I've been waiting for your call, Tyrone," she responded.

He was shocked, and could feel his heart pounding with the beats coming consistently faster.

"Would you please tell me how you knew that I was going to call?" he demanded.

"No time to explain that right now," she replied.

Ty became impatient, hoping for a quick resolution, but there was no chance of that happening; nothing was going to be resolved at that point.

The lady directed him to go immediately to Western Union and send her $80 and a number where he could be reached. She also wanted him to procure some white candles of a certain size. She was very specific about what to do with each candle. The way she sounded, so self-assured, all Ty's second guessing went right out the window. Even though Jackie was laughing and taunting him, he continued to write down all of the information the healer provided.

Jackie was telling him how stupid he was to go and give money to someone he didn't even know. He had his own doubts, but those doubts didn't concern what he was going through, or had been through, he was very sure of that. He had one hour to conduct this transaction. The clock was ticking; the ultimatum had been laid down from both sides.

Ty hung the phone up knowing he didn't have the money to do this. But he would get it. With his plans set, he got dressed and then attempted to cool things down before leaving. While driving away from the old house, he worried about Caroline, about leaving her there in that awful place. He knew he had some time, but not much. There was always a pause after each horrible battle.

Tyrone drove to the nearest phone booth and called Rene, talked for a minute, and then asked to speak to Steve. He couldn't go into details as to why he needed the money, just that he would pay it back as soon as he could. Steve said it would be okay, so Ty drove directly to his house and borrowed the money. Now, with the money situation in hand, the next stop was the shopping mall with a Western Union and a place where Ty could get the candles he needed. Everything was working like clockwork. Ty was all charged up inside but very calm-looking on the outside.

When he got out of the car at the mall, it felt as if someone or something their was watching him—and following him closely. Ty just kept talking to himself, vowing not to show any fear or weakness. He knew he looked run down, but he carried it off, praying he wouldn't run into anyone he knew. All Ty wanted was to get in and out of that store as fast as he could.

But it didn't turn out that way.

Ty stood at the counter for ten minutes waiting for help, and started becoming a little uneasy, counting the money and checking the address over and over again. He was thinking about the time, wondering compulsively if he had enough.

When help finally came, the store clerk was unsure of how to process the paper work and needed assistance. The pressure suddenly became intense. The scare grew worse than the way things started that morning. What a big let-down! Ty's mind was running wild again. The positive thoughts were slipping away and negative notions ran out of control. After standing in one place for so long, he was stressed out but still trying to suppress it. All of a sudden, the building seemed to become unsettled.

Patches of darkness, like shadows, were appearing inside the building high up on the walls. Ty didn't want to focus on anything, however. He just kept looking down, pretending to be interested in the contents of the glass counter he was leaning on. He needed the help of the Higher Power and that healer now more then ever.

Then Ty began talking to himself, wondering what was going on. It was his time, the Higher Power knew what he had done; was he going to be all right? Ty was ready! This conversation with himself had been going on for some time now.

Finally the store clerk returned with help, and business was taken care of. Now for the candles. He went up and down the aisles until he located the candles he needed, and then got in line to pay for them. While he was standing there, he could hear a rumbling sound.

Ty looked up nervously as if the building was going to collapse. High up on the wall were two great round, dark shapes, figures with feline eyes. Caught off guard he could not believe what he appeared to be seeing. So instead he sought a reflection of something that could possibly be creating those shadows so high up on the wall—far above everything else.

The eye contact that Ty and those figures were having was so real to him. The blinking of the eyes on that wall convinced Ty that anger and hostility were filling the store. He was overwhelmed with fear and his heart was racing again. Ty hated it when his heart beat this hard because it felt like he was fighting off a seizure.

He began sweating profusely and feared the extreme fright might stop his heart. If anything was going to happen, though, he wanted it to go down in front of all these people congregating at the mall. Then his terror abated and he started getting mad. His lips were moving and Ty actually started speaking out loud. He realized then that he had lost faith and was losing self-control in turn. He hung tough. There was only one person in line ahead of him, and knowing that soon it would be his turn to get out of that store, strengthened him further. He put his head down again, hoping he didn't look guilty or suspicious, and smiled as he finally greeted the check-out girl.

Once Ty finally got out he headed for a phone booth. His heart was still racing and he had to catch his breath before dialing the number. As he dialed, he began chanting: "Come on, come on, be there." His part was done. He wanted to give the lady the confirmation number so she could verify the transaction and get to work on his problem.

She answered the phone.

"Hello!"

"Hello. You made it," she said in a cheerful, congratulatory manner.

She then gave Ty his next series of instructions and bid him good-bye. He hung up the phone, but instead of going back to the old Newton house, he drove to Steve and Rene's house, where he thought it would be best to complete his next tasks and call the lady back in two hours as he had been instructed.

Ty showed up at Steve and Rene's looking like a bit of a wild man, complete with bulging eyes and a sore neck from swiveling his head so wildly during the fifteen minute drive. Rene was the first to meet him when he pulled up at their house, but he didn't catch too much of what she had to say.

Ty just ran off at the mouth, babbling at high speed. He confused her then locked himself up in their garage. It was dark. He hurriedly lit the candles and sat down on the floor, sitting as close to the tiny flames as he could get. Ty attempted to sit perfectly still, trying not to think about all the dark corners in the garage. There was so much stuff in there that if he stared at anything for any length of time it could be completely re-shaped by the darkness and Ty's imagination. To make matters worse, Rene had recovered herself and was now knocking at the door wanting in, demanding to know what he was doing. Ty became very disturbed and nervous. He knew at any time that Rene could open the door with her key if she really wanted to.

Ty could not open the door—he had to be in here by himself with these candles lit for an hour with absolutely no disturbances. It had been made clear to him by the lady in New Jersey and it was vitally important. His life depended on everything going perfectly from the time he made the first call back east. So no matter what, he was not going to open that door. He was also supposed to be very quiet. The clock was ticking and the longer he remained in there, the more persistent Rene became, standing outside the door. Ty didn't know what she thought he was doing but he did know that she was putting their lives in serious danger by trying to make conversation.

Finally, Ty's time in this dark garage was over. It had been miserable due to all of the distraction Rene had been causing. Coming out, he first tried to gather his nerves and then his thoughts, but had no problem with maintaining faith in what he was doing. Dealing with Rene, however, was something he worried about. What was he going to tell her? He couldn't give her details, that was for sure. Actually he wanted to belt her right in the mouth, but he had to do as he had been told to do. Talking out loud about how to handle unwanted spiritual matters was not the thing to do.

He apologized for upsetting her, and explained that he had badly needed some time to sort out some things that were bothering him.

"I was more or less meditating with a candle lit in a spiritual way throughout that past hour," he explained.

"Wow!" Rene responded. "I didn't know what to think. Is everything going to be okay?"

"Well, in the long run I'm hoping everything will work itself out, but don't worry, Rene," Ty answered, adding that he had a phone call to make.

"Have you eaten this morning?" Rene asked.

"No."

"Well come on inside. Steve is in here cooking breakfast," she said, trying to recover from Ty's arrival.

They went inside the house, where Ty had very little to say. He just waited, and anticipated the phone call he had to make.

Steve carried on a little conversation while everyone ate. He pretty much knew what was on Ty's mind. With less than 30 minutes to go, he felt he already knew what was going to be said, but needed to know if he had been taking his mind too far, or was right on the money with all that had happened, and what was going to happen next.

The time of waiting was up. Ty dried his sweaty palms, picked up the phone and dialed the number.

"Hello, it's me…returning the call. It's been two hours," he said.

The lady told Ty to sit down and relax. He was not to say a word, just listen. Whatever she would say, Ty repeated it out loud until she stopped him and firmly told him not to repeat another word aloud. He knew repeating all of what she was saying out loud so that Steve and Rene would be in on the conversation was wrong and dangerous, but her words were frightening and Ty didn't want to keep all of this to himself.

First of all, this person, this lady (or perhaps his Confidante now), was someone he had never seen, met, or even heard of before in his life. And now for this someone, Confidante, to tell him step-by-step, year-by-year, what had taken place in his life, in his family's life, past and present was terrifying Ty. Ready or not, he was willing to believe in what this lady had to say about his future. As he continued to listen to the Confidante, she told him more of what she knew about his situation.

Ty began crying when the Confidante told him about an article that the boys had found on the property at the old house.

"Boy Hurt In Blast Shoots Self Dead (June 25, 1923— Associated Press) Monterey, CA. Joseph Hillzer, 8, Commits Suicide After Painful Injury." Joseph, it seems, was a precocious child, having already passed the eighth grade examination at his tender age. On that June day in 1923 the eight-year-old found a dynamite cap near his house that had been left behind by a grading crew. It exploded, leaving him badly wounded. He managed to make it home with his sister, trying to stop his bleeding. Unable to face disfigurement for the rest of his life, the boy went into the house, retrieved a .32 caliber revolver from his mother's dresser and shot himself though the heart.

At this point, Ty began showing some real signs of losing control. Rene started to cry. Steve held her, telling her not to worry. As the pressure built within Ty, he came closer and closer to yelling out, going crazy. There was no longer any possibility of a practical joke or drug induced fancies. Joseph Hillzer had experienced some 75 years of existence on this earth as a lost soul. Ty was now expecting the worst from his Confidante's conversation.

"Do you remember *The Exorcist*?" she asked him.

"Yes," he said. "No! Oh please no," Ty yelled before she could continue and then he started crying again completely out of control and totally disgusted.

Rene and Steve now demanded to know what was going on.

"What in hell is going on?" they demanded in unison.

Ty could hear his Confidante on the phone over Rene and Steve's insistent interruptions. "Who else is there? Get yourself together, have some control," she whispered urgently. "You must do as I am telling you, or else you will be in some insane institution for the remaining days of your life with everyone thinking you are crazy. And then would come the fatal blow from that lost soul," the Confidante added.

Ty believed truly that the old house was an evil hole where a platoon of lost and unwanted souls resided. Just one of the many cabals of Satanism that appear throughout our world controlled by the one called Lord of the Flies, the master evil spirit and the great adversary of mankind.

"What is this spirit's main objective here?" Ty asked his Confidante.

"Ty, that evil spirit wants eternal life through your virgin child and he can obtain that by taking Caroline's virginity from her and killing her instantly," the Confidante answered.

"This young evil spirit has indulged in Jackie, controlling her, becoming overwhelmed with her womb, and now wants a virgin for himself," Ty blurted out, mad, scared, and out of control.

Steve told him to calm down as he was scaring Rene to death.

Confidante made it loud and clear that Ty had been chosen to put this lost soul to rest. He had no choice. Whatever the case, this conversation had already gone way too far. Ty did not know what to say, do, or think. Confidante told him when to call again, and said that he would be guided regarding what to do step by step, day by day. Ty gave her Steve's mailing address. She had things coming Ty's way via next day airmail. All he could feel was a sense of urgency, knowing this problem was greater than life itself. Ty was a wreck, knowing Jackie would remain in a vulnerable position unless she on her own showed faith, and ask to be saved. There could be no turning back. Ty hung in there for the remainder of the phone call.

After he hung up, however, he again began crying, and remained unable to talk about it. It was very hard, especially for someone who likes to talk. He was just scared, and growing numb. Ty knew the next move was his to make, but wasn't ready to do anything just yet. He started trying to think of reasons and excuses why he should not have to deal with the problem he was already so intimately involved with.

Steve tried to help as best he could under the circumstances, but he did not know what the Confidante had Ty.

"I'm not going to guess about anything that has to be done, and that's the truth," Ty vowed to himself.

Ty started walking around inside the house reading over the list of things he had to obtain before the next conversation with his Confidante in two days. In the meantime, Ty told Steve and Rene not to worry, and that he would work with Steve in the morning but must get back to Caroline and Jackie at the old house. Ty dreaded going there and having to answer any questions from Jackie, but he was just going to more or less lie to her. He couldn't trust her, or take a chance on revealing anything to her of the things he had believed all along.

Steve and Rene walked Ty out to the car, gave him a hug and told him to be careful, and to call if he needed anything.

Ty drove back to the old house feeling stronger, less afraid, and a little angrier now that things were out in the open. There was no more wondering what was going on. Plus, his Confidante had told him that she was going back into the church right away to begin the meditation and prayer. The candlelight vigil was also in effect, and there was going to be a shield in place around Ty's family for a time. His faith was now invested in the Confidante.

When Ty drove up to the old house, he wasn't surprise to see that Jackie was still at home. The way she looked early this morning he had a feeling she wasn't going anywhere, not even the normal Sunday outing with her mother. He doubted she was going to be exactly herself either.

As soon as he walked into the house, Ty did his best to make it seem as if all was well. Of course, Jackie wanted to know what had gone on. Ty kept his responses short, but did say that changes needed to be made and that they would talk about it later. It was getting close to dinner time, Ty hadn't had lunch and he was hungry.

"Would you like to take the kids to get something fast for dinner?" he asked Jackie.

She responded in a solemn, unemotional fashion. "You can go and get the kids something to eat if you want to."

Jason and Ben heard Ty, and came out of their room, anxious to go; so did Caroline. Ty felt he needed to get going right away, as he sensed that Jackie wanted to pick a fight.

Jason, Ben, Caroline and Ty got in Ty's car and left. They stayed gone long enough so that when they got back to the house it would be time to get Caroline ready for bed.

Ty also kept himself occupied before going to bed by preparing for work, and feeding Cass and changing her bandages. He was not going to let his guard down, paying close attention to Jackie and the house itself. Caroline got herself all tucked into bed, and waited for Ty to finish what he was doing so he could read a little to her and kiss her good night.

The boys didn't have any school the next day. Ty went into their room to let them know that he wanted the leaves that had been raked into piles in the yard picked up before they left the house.

He came out of their room and Jackie had already turned off the TV and the lights. He did want to at least try and talk to Jackie but she had lain down in bed next to Caroline acting as if she had been asleep for hours.

So much for that. Ty checked and made sure everything was locked up, and then he got comfortable on the floor and lay very still in the dark.

The next morning he didn't remember hearing anything throughout the night. He had been mentally drained, and the extra stress thinking about Jackie right before he fell asleep wiped him out for the night. Jackie remained locked in that solemn mood she was in, so Ty helped Caroline get ready for school, and left the house without even saying good-bye.

He dropped Caroline off at school and headed to Steve's house. Steve had the trucks warmed up and ready to go when Ty pulled up.

"Good morning," Steve said.

"Good morning. How is Rene?" Ty replied.

Steve knew from Ty's tone of voice that he wanted to pass on any questions regarding the previous night.

"Rene did fine after you left yesterday, and she's already at work this morning," Steve answered.

At work Ty stayed busy and didn't say much up until it was time to leave. Steve told him before he left the job that he could always talk to him if he needed to. Ty thanked him and left to pick up Caroline from school.

Caroline and Ty came home to find the leaves still piled in the yard. He walked into the house and into the boy's room. "Why didn't the leaves get picked up today?" he demanded.

Jason replied with a smart answer. "I didn't have to pick them up."

Ty was surprised by Jason's reply. He knew that the boy was acting out because his cousin Raymond was there. Raymond managed to always stay in some kind of mischief. He reminded Ty of himself at times when Ty was a kid.

Jason and Ty began to argue while Ben lay quietly in the top bunk, and Raymond stood by the bedroom door. Caroline also stood close by, listening. The argument soon got out of control.

Ty became furious after Jason told him that again he was not going to pick up any leaves, and he was splitting no matter what Ty had to say. He also informed Ty that the older man would have to take on all three of the boys if he tried to stop them. Ty had heard and seen a lot of crazy things go on at this old house, but now he had heard it all.

He backed out of the boys' room, picked up the phone, and dialed Jackie's work number. As the phone rang, he told Jason that they all had better get ready because he was coming back.

Jackie answered the phone and Ty began shouting about how Jason had spoken to him. Ty also told her that if she could not talk some sense into him over the phone, she had better come home right away. Instead of backing him up, however, she made Ty more upset. Ty then threatened the boys, and Jackie handed the phone to a fellow employee in hopes of calming Ty down while she rushed home.

By the time Jackie arrived at the house the boys and Ty had already started a fist fight. Raymond was the first to jump on Ty, followed by Ben. As Jackie pulled up in front of the house, Ben and Raymond were standing outside looking scared to death. The boys had taken on more than they could handle.

Jackie walked through the front door to find the house in ruins. Jason had gotten hurt badly. Jackie went for the phone to call the police and Ty knew that he was in big trouble. He was on probation already, and if the police came he was headed to jail for a long time.

Ty began explaining to Jackie what had happened once again, and asked her not to get the police involved. She put the phone down, and attended to Jason.

Ty went out into the back yard and sat down to cool off. When he came back into the house, she asked him to pack all of his belonging and leave the house for good. Ty called Steve and told him what had happened. Steve and Rene came over right away and brought a truck. Jackie was so upset she called Carla, who also showed up. Everything was a mess. Jackie and Caroline were crying. Carla and Rene helped clean up the house while Steve put the back door back on its hinges. Ty hated that it had happened like this, but there was nothing he could do to change it now.

They continued to load the truck with not only Ty's things, but Caroline's as well. Ty had no intention of leaving her at this house with Jackie. The things that got broken were taken outside and the rest of their belongings were stacked in the truck. Ty stayed tough, but the thought of leaving Jackie at this house by herself hurt and it didn't help with Jackie and Caroline continuing to cry while Steve's truck pulled away from the old house with Ty and Caroline.

It was a long and slow ride to Steve and Rene's house. Ty sat quietly in the truck hurting over having had to leave Cass behind. She hadn't healed yet and Jackie had asked if she could stay. Ty left her only because Jackie said that she would feel safer if Cass remained. His day had been tough, and it seemed like that old house had gotten the best of him by separating him and Jackie. Ty wanted to cry when he left, but keeping the faith was the main thing and staying positive for Caroline.

Ty was worn out; things just didn't seem like they were going to get any better right away, but as quiet as it was kept, he was glad to have gotten Caroline away from that house on Newton St.

Chapter 10

It was late by the time Steve and Ty unloaded the contents of the truck into Steve's garage. Rene took Caroline inside and got her cleaned up and fed. Steve and Ty came in soon after, grabbed a bite to eat and then Caroline and Ty bedded down. Everyone had to deal with work and school the next day.

Some time later, Steve and Rene noticed that Ty's light was still on and they tentatively entered his room.

"What are you doing up? Is everything going to be all right?" she asked him.

Ty smiled for the first time in a while. "With the help and faith I have in the Higher Power, I'm going to be all right," he assured her. "Right now, it's important for me to start writing down my entire experiences, from the beginning, so everyone in the world for the rest of time can read about it."

"Okay," Rene agreed. "Maybe that's a good idea."

Steve had once mentioned that he had kept a diary. Ty hadn't paid close attention to Steve's story at the time, but he believed him. Ty, on the other hand, still couldn't let his story out, knowing it would bring only harm to Steve and Rene. It was bad enough staying in their house with the evil entities from Newton St. seeking Caroline's soul and Ty's life. Ty was taking this more seriously than simply writing a diary for himself. No, this very first line on the very first page of his writing would signal the start of a crucial process. At least that's what was going through Ty's mind. They all said good night and finally slept.

Ty woke up the next morning feeling that he had actually gotten some rest for a change. He felt good. Caroline was also well-rested and looking forward to school. She gave Ty a hug and didn't mention anything about the day before as she prepared to leave.

Steve was already up and had seen Rene off to work. He told Ty that he had made them breakfast and then had to go check out a job. He would meet Ty back at the house after Caroline had been taken to school.

Ty and Caroline were driving toward the schoolyard when Caroline quietly asked Ty to check on her mom when he got back to Steve's house.

"Of course I will, Caroline. Just don't worry. Everything is going to be okay! You aren't the only one who's worried about mom," he assured her. "I'll call mom at work. And remember, you are not to worry," he reminded her. Caroline smiled as she got out of the car.

When Ty got back to Steve's house he was alone. He quickly gathered himself before making a phone call to Jackie's work. He had to be careful what he said or asked; he didn't want to set her off and have to deal with her new split personality.

When he called, Jackie answered.

"Are you okay?" Ty asked.

"Yes," she said. "But I would like Caroline to stay at the old house with me this coming weekend," she added.

Ty did not respond. He just played it off and changed the subject. He told her that he loved her and added that Caroline missed and loved mommy too. Steve had pulled up in front of the house and honked the horn, breaking the silence. Ty assured Jackie that he would make sure Caroline called before she went to bed.

"I've got to go," he said.

"Good-bye," she responded flatly.

The day went by pretty quickly. The work kept Ty's mind largely intact in spite of the anticipation regarding the package he would be receiving from the Confidante the following morning.

The first thing Caroline asked about, as soon as she got into the car, was her mom's condition. Ty told her that her mom was fine, and that she could not wait to hear from Caroline. He told Caroline that she could call Jackie before she went to bed that night. Caroline settled down after hearing that.

They returned to Steve and Rene's house, where Rene was waiting with snacks for Caroline. Those two spent the rest of the afternoon together, and Ty got himself cleaned up and found a corner in the house where he began writing until Steve came home.

Ty then went outside and helped Steve put away some tools and equipment. They talked a little about Jackie, Caroline and Rene. Ty was pleased to hear that Rene was okay with him and Caroline staying until they could find their own place to stay. Steve was also happy to know that he had made contact with Jackie and that Caroline would be able to talk with her later that night.

Ty told Steve he would not be working in the morning. Steve understood and told him to handle whatever it was he needed to do. In fact, Ty ended up not working much at all because he needed to concentrate on the matter at hand.

After dinner he read Caroline a story then let her call Jackie to say good night. Ty didn't get on the phone; he simply told Caroline to tell mom that he loved her and would talk to her tomorrow.

Ty couldn't wait until 10:00 the next morning. He hurried Caroline to school, and hurried back to Steve's house and waited for the package to arrive.

When the package got there, Ty called his Confidante. She answered the phone and took him slowly through the contents of the package, carefully explaining each item, and what he was to do with them.

She told him that this was the beginning of the cleansing of his soul. Everything was new to him; Ty did not know much about any of what she was talking about, but he was definitely taking notes.

Inside the package were dissolving crystals for Ty's bath water and a few small, round, white candles. She instructed Ty to burn one of the candles every 15 minutes during each bath. Also, there were two thick round candles in different colors; these candles also had their purpose, and their time for burning, she explained.

Just so you know, the thick candles most definitely will have an effect on the bad spirits. Believe it. You will know when the bad spirits are around and when they aren't," she assured him.

There was also a prayer book in the packet entitled, "Sacred Heart."

She then became more direct with him, explaining that the evil spirit's teeth had been sunk into him and his family, and in a matter of time—a short time—it would be all over. "All right, all over for you," she said. "You cannot make any mistakes; everything has to be at a certain time. Your writing, your phone calls to me and to Jackie, and bedtimes too. You are no longer going to be in control of what you do each day. I am accepting no excuses. Your life depends on your every move."

Her lecture had gotten too intense for Ty and he had to interrupt her.

"Please! Give me a minute," he pleaded.

When Ty first called this lady, and let her in on what was going on, he believed it would be the end of his worries. She would handle his problems with just a few tricks of her trade, and it would all be over! Now Ty knew he had thought wrong.

"Are you still there?" his Confidante asked.

"Yes," he answered.

"If you have anything you want to ask me, you need to ask it now," she warned.

"What should I do about Jackie wanting Caroline to visit her at the old house?" Ty immediately asked.

His Confidante, however, answered all his questions by saying no to anything that involved Jackie or that old house. She insisted Jackie and Ty were better off away from each other, but that Jackie was safe when Ty was not around her.

"Why?"

"The young evil spirit and Jackie are roommates. They do everything together. She is his woman."

She put it to him hard, and insisted he was not safe anywhere. Ty was worried, and scared, and like a typical man, he could not stand the fact that the young spirit Joseph was having sex with Jackie.

"I'm to abandon her and run?" he asked.

"No, but you and your family will die sooner than you can imagine if you don't listen."

She told Ty she would guide him when it came time to do what he was supposed to do about Jackie. "As far as the good night calls for Caroline, let Jackie be the one who calls, and when you talk to her keep it short and sweet.

"Whether you like it or not, Jackie is your enemy. She doesn't know it. She has no control. The young spirit is working through her to get to Caroline, and to destroy you," the Confidante said.

She promised that she would be on alert, and that she would keep a shield over Jackie as best she could. The Confidante said that she needed more time, good time in church, no interruption while meditating, praying and conducting candlelight vigils. She would be watching over Ty and his family day in and day out. Ty was told it was too late to be worrying about male pride while he was not at that old house, because the spectral rape had happened right in his face when he was there.

"Be grateful to be alive and get back focused on what got you to this point," the Confidante said.

She needed for Ty to use his abilities. She was amazed at what he had accomplished on his own thus far. She needed Ty's help; she wanted him to write when she instructed him to, since she could draw energy from it and learn more from Ty about this strange situation.

The coming of the Exorcist in the year 2000. I cannot let this happen to myself or my family, Ty vowed. It was a must that he remains strong and keep the faith in what he believes is right.

Ty was gifted and blessed with strong visions at the outer limit of one's beliefs, and Confidante felt strongly about that, she admitted.

"I do not have a choice in the matter; I have known this for a while. I have been ready to fight, but truthfully, I don't like the idea of being some kind of ghost buster and I am not feeling remotely heroic from any of this." Ty declared.

"And when you think about it, my chances right now are slim to none," he told her. "And I think slim just left town."

"Only if you fail to follow my lead," she said sternly. "Your every move needs to be made with care."

She was telling it like it was. Ty was quiet and listened to her. Ultimately, he gave her his word that he was with her, all the way. He really did understand the importance of this whole thing. "It's real and I know it," he said.

"I would know if you are with me or not," the Confidante assured him. "It has a lot to do with the timing of things to come," she went on, but those were the last words she spoke before setting the time for their next phone conversation. Ty didn't want to hang up, but it was time.

He needed to get his head together for the time when he would light the candles, and do all the things he had to do in Rene's house. She really wasn't much on having spiritual rituals performed in her home. She didn't like any kind of burning of anything in her place.

Ty knew he was going to need a place for himself and Caroline so he could have his space and privacy. He went through the same routine that evening with Caroline, getting her homework completed, and cleaned up, except, she read to Auntie Rene while Ty took a bath.

Rene told Ty when he came out of the bathroom that Jackie had called while he was soaking in the tub. Ty hadn't spoken to Jackie at all that day. He had no plans of calling her back as long as she said goodnight to Caroline. That was all that mattered. Anyway, everything went fine. Ty felt safe although the surroundings outside seemed a little strange. It didn't bother him though. He kissed and hugged Caroline as she lay quietly in bed.

Ty pulled a chair up next to the bed and began to write a little. He was very tired; the hot bath had made him so relaxed he could barely stay awake. He said a prayer and turned the lights out early.

The next morning Rene and Steve awoke in a jocular mood for some reason. Caroline and Ty walked into the kitchen, and Rene started talking about all the noises she had heard last night outside her bedroom window. Steve agreed there were noises. They started joking about something strange outside moving things around in the backyard.

Ty joined in and made a few amusing remarks so that Caroline wouldn't take the discussion seriously. He didn't want her being afraid and staying awake during the next few nights.

When Caroline left the room to go wash up for breakfast, Steve and Rene started kidding again, one joke after another and Ty just laughed along, totally bemused.

"No, we are not joking," Steve finally admitted. "We lay in bed last night and listened to all the strange sounds that were going on outside in our backyard. Our dog was also pacing and growling at the movements and the sounds. We really did hear a lot of weird things going on that never happened before at our house."

He simply could not tell them that the good spirits summoned by the Confidante were watching over everyone in their house last night, but he was happy to know that Rene and Steve had been aware of something unusual. The Confidante had told Ty that he would rest well and to have no worries because the good spirits would be all around them. Ty couldn't wait to take Caroline to school and for Steve and Rene to go to work so he could light the candle as he had been instructed.

After finishing his various tasks, Ty spent the rest of the morning seeking an apartment. He ended up staying with Steve and Rene for the entire month of April, during which Caroline and Ty didn't see much of Jackie.

Jackie did come by on Ty's birthday and they all went out for dinner. She didn't stay for desert, but left suddenly. So, Ty went on and had plenty to drink. He wanted to go and behave badly with her but was relieved when she left. It would have been so easy to go and get high with her had she stayed longer, especially after drinking as much as he did. It had been awful. She acted like she hated him. Still, he had been warned by the Confidante that it would be that way. How could he blame her? He kept Caroline from going anywhere with her and Jackie rarely got to talk to Caroline. It was meant to be one of the worst nights ever and that was all there was to it.

Ty knew that young spirit was at the old house waiting for him but he was not in any shape to watch him play with Jackie, so that didn't happen.

Ty knew that keeping Steve and Rene in the middle was getting old. He could sense as time passed that they wanted their space and privacy as badly as he wanted to give it to them.

Ty finally found an apartment. It happened right on time because things weren't looking so good based on as his last conversation with the Confidante. Ty and his Confidante were going to need a lot more time, working together, so the apartment privacy was welcomed.

Chapter 11

A lot of stress accompanied the moving. They had to turn on the electricity, connect the phone and buy all new furniture for the apartment. Ty was also thinking about Cass and Caroline and not being able to spend time with Jackie. He was awaiting the arrival of the second package from his Confidante, as well. The family got settled over the weekend quite quickly.

Ty returned to the apartment after taking Caroline to school and the second package arrived at the apartment soon thereafter. He made the call and got his Confidante on the phone.

She grabbed his attention quickly by telling him that now was the time to bless the apartment, to prepare it for the "worst to come." She sent him some holy water, a very nice rosary to wear around his neck, some more candles, and a crucifix to straddle the entrance way of his apartment. As Ty was going through these things, the Confidante was explaining each item just as she had with the first package at Rene's house.

He interrupted her by asking: "How serious is this 'worst to come'? What do you mean by that exactly?"

She promised to finish going over the details with him and when she was done, she would explain what was happening. It was getting a little tense for Ty, looking into the package, there were a lot of things that had yet to be gone over, and he didn't have any idea what these objects were for. He took a deep breath and listened carefully.

The Confidante explained that the package included several rocks and that each rock served a purpose. One was for Caroline; it was very smooth and white. It had a very warm and soft feeling about it. It was to go everywhere Caroline went, the woman instructed. It was a must that Caroline kept it and no one else was to touch it at all. When she slept, it was to be underneath her. It would bring the child very pleasant dreams and keep the evil spirits from harming her. Ty was very touched by this object.

Ty's rock, however, was strong, massive in feeling, and he felt every bit of the stone's power to block evil from his path. It would embolden Ty's approach and outlook on this entire matter the instant she finished explaining it. Instantly, Ty was ready to huff and puff just like the Big Bad Wolf and blow that house down. The rock was to be in his pocket at all times. It would help with his confidence.

There were other crystals and stones which were to be put around in and on top of things in each room in the apartment. Last was a list of things he had to pick up from a store. Ty needed three amethyst crystals, and, as always, more candles.

The mysterious woman finished explaining the details of how long and when to burn the candles, and the time for Ty to write, how long and where. He had gone from one extreme to the other— from smoking rocks to hiding rocks and burning candles. But Ty just wanted this whole nightmare to end. He also wanted to hear more about the evil spirit—the boy named Joseph. She explained that Ty's name was not recognized in any church nor had he been going to any church. Ty put two and two together.

"Oh, boy! I know what that means. The young evil spirit is going to come at Caroline and me full force every nightfall, right?" he asked.

"Correct," she replied. Ty was feeling weaker than sweet water.

"I'm more than ready to get prepared," Ty replied.

With the help of the Confidante, Ty prepared the bedroom. He took white training tape one-and-a-half inches wide and made crosses. He put the white crosses all over on both sides of the door, high and low, on the head of the bed and the foot of the bed; on the closet doors, on the bathroom door, on the cabinet door, and under the bathroom sink. He made one big cross for underneath the bed.

Now his Confidante instructed him to strengthen the crosses by putting holy water on each cross in all the corners of the room. He was to bless that room well, and pray for strength and courage. Ty told her that he would be sure to have candles in the bedroom.

Then their phone conversation was over. Ty had gotten all of the instructions that he needed for now. It was time for him to take off and acquire the rest of the things on the list. Once he picked up Caroline from school and ate, cleaned up, and got Caroline's homework done, there would be no time for anything else. He was going to make sure they were locked up in their room before it got dark. That was going to be the plan for weeks to come.

Ty was driving toward the mall wondering about the effect all this might have on Caroline—the way their room was fixed up and her having to carry a special rock at all times. Even though Ty felt Caroline was just as in tune as he was to what was happening, and that she was cool and understood everything that had taken place at the old house, he still didn't want to scare Caroline with the stone and all. She did have to carry the rock. He thought about this for a while and decided to wait for the best time to talk to her.

Ty was going to wait until they were in bed that night. She liked the idea of getting into bed early because that meant more books would be read to her. That night, Ty explained everything to her as simply and calmly as he could. He always assured her that the Higher Power was with both of them and they needed to follow the Higher Power's ways.

So he introduced Caroline to the rock.

"This rock is very special, it is for you," he said. "It is from the Higher Power and He asked me to ask you if you would take care of His gift to you. It will make you feel warm and happy and keep you thinking good thoughts. Now this is a secret between the Higher Power and you and Daddy," he told her. "Can you keep a secret from the evil spirits and—everyone else?" he asked.

"Yes," she said.

"You aren't the only one that got a special rock. Daddy got a special rock too and I am going to do the same as you. I am not going to tell anyone."

Caroline kept an eye on her rock from that night onward. The two slept in white undershirts and bottoms on top of the covers with the light on in the room and in the bathroom all night. Every night Ty and his candles made it seem bright as daytime in their room at all times.

It was the month of May, 1997. They had put their faith and trust in the Higher Power. It was serious as life and death. Each night Ty reclined in bed with the phone by his side. He could call his Confidante if needed, but she was the last person he would speak to on a nightly basis. He did not want to talk to anyone else, either, and would not answer the phone if he did not hear the code that he and his Confidante had agreed upon after their last good night and prayers were spoken.

Ty would lie there in bed, holding his rock with the rosary around his neck, just thinking how he was in a fight, and battling back his tears. He would try hard to stay awake because he wanted to keep an eye on Caroline as well as the room. It was as if every move was countered with another move, and he couldn't be content with the fact that he was bathed in light all night. Still, after the way they had prepared the room, he had no reason to fear.

Ty clung to that belief, but it still wasn't enough because sooner or later he knew he was going to be tested with one of Joseph's most powerful weapons.

He had failed in every attempt so far. Joseph was getting smarter every day. Ty knew his enemy was waiting for the right time to strike at them in the new apartment. He would be waiting for Ty's guard to drop, just a little. He was also waiting for Ty and Jackie to start partying.

Ty clenched his fists, swearing that would not happen. He was going to hold out as long as he could. In fact, he had other plans. He was fired up on adrenaline but tired as well and he needed to close his eyes and trust. It was time to demonstrate his faith.

When he woke up the next day, Ty felt well-rested. He had begun preparing himself and Caroline for church that weekend at the Church of Christ, where he had worshiped as a young boy. They made it to church Sunday morning and it was a good feeling as Ty was reacquainted with members of the church from his past attendance. He was a bit excited and proud with Caroline by his side. He also had in mind that he was not leaving this church without a Bible. He didn't have one and decided the best place to borrow one was from the church. Ty asked for and was given a Bible.

Once church was over, Ty and Caroline made it to the car complete with their new Bible. Ty believed he had won the first week after making all the right moves in their new apartment.

The days and nights became redundant by the second week. Ty read the Bible every night to Caroline. Jackie called the apartment and, surprisingly, the phone conversation went smoothly. Jackie was going to meet Caroline and Ty at their new apartment for the first time next Sunday after they returned from church. Things were really going in Ty's favor. He then felt certain that he had won the first week.

Caroline was very excited to see Jackie when she arrived at the apartment door. She came in for a few minutes. Ty gave her a hug and she commented on how nicely the apartment was decorated. Ty didn't show her the bedroom; that door was always closed.

Jackie told him she would bring Caroline back later, and not to worry because she would definitely not take her to the old house, she added sarcastically. Ty did not comment, pretending he did not hear her. He only agreed to this visit because she was taking Caroline to visit grandma's and then go shopping.

Ty was relieved when they left and wanted to share it with his Confidante. He called her and they stayed on the phone until Jackie and Caroline returned.

Caroline walked through the front door just as Ty was hanging up the phone.

"Where is mom?" he asked Caroline.

"She is leaving, she dropped me off," Caroline explained.

Ty ran out to the sidewalk and barely got a wave off as Jackie drove away. He came back inside the apartment trying not to show that he was hurt because he didn't get a chance to say good-bye to her. Maybe it was for the best, he thought.

Ty began making dinner but Caroline wasn't hungry, so he made himself something to eat as Caroline talked about how she spent the day with her mom and grandma.

Darkness was closing fast. They hustled and got all cleaned up and into bed before nightfall. Ty read the Bible first, and then he read a couple of Caroline's favorite stories until she began to drift off to sleep. Then he lay back, wiping the sweat off of his forehead. He had been holding back so much fear and discomfort while reading to Caroline. He gathered himself and replayed the conversation he had with his Confidante earlier.

"Ty, tonight the evil will line your apartment roof top, black as crows, bringing nothing but hoodoo, hanging like bats. There will be a skeleton head place on your center table right outside your room door. Whatever you do, don't open that door. You won't be alone; there will be good spirits in there to fight the infested room full of evil. The confrontations, battles, will be ungovernable. You are to close your eyes, have faith and pray yourself to sleep. Tomorrow morning you are to act as if you never heard this conversation and ask nothing of it, and carry on with your new task." She had scheduled a few changes in his daytime activities, and vowed to begin them the very next day.

The next morning while Caroline was in school, Ty set out for the beach. The Confidante wanted him to write at the beach and walk in the ocean waters to cleanse himself. He did just that and it evoked the feeling of something much greater than the life all around him. He was getting so much closer to what he really felt.

He observed the powerful formation of the waves washing down on him. He was nervous at first, but he came there in peace looking for a connection, a direct connection to help wash away his sins. The water reached his ankles, which were penetrated with pain as he stood listening to the ocean speak in a masterful way. He accepted the pain from the surging waters that engulfed his feet. He cried, and then smiled, and rejoiced as he felt that unwanted feeling—the feeling which that evil young spirit had cast upon his soul—leave his body.

Each day as the month of May neared its end, he stood on this shallow ocean floor, when he was not standing on it, he was sitting in the sands staring out at the ocean with pencil in hand, going freely on its own, writing away.

Ty was identifying with the evil spirit's weakness. He now knew why he was so clear in his thoughts. He felt a connection with the water as he wrote. He did not have that same connection, or feeling, when he wrote where there wasn't any water. It was like church. He felt safe. He felt the same here at the beach standing in the water. Now this was a big deal to Tyrone. But the most important thing was the knowledge that religion was no myth. He was living it, experiencing it. That's what was keeping him alive. So, here he was, excited, knowing that he was part of this team. He had faith; he was bringing something to the table. He was helping in the fight against evil.

Ty lay back in the sand and praised the skies above. It was great to know he had a Confidante on his side as well as the Almighty, of course. He prayed to the Higher Power. He couldn't wait until it was time to call his Confidante this evening and share what he had experienced.

He left the beach affirming to himself that he was worthy of being saved, and could even help others. Once Caroline and Ty got back to the apartment, it was the same routine. He would be looking over both shoulders while they got everything together before darkness fell.

That night Caroline wanted to call Jackie to say good night. She did so and then Ty spoke to Jackie for several minutes. Ty told her that he loved her very much. They said they would be together soon and Caroline let out a sigh of happiness knowing that daddy still loved mom. They both said goodnight one last time before hanging up.

Caroline and Ty spoke to each other for a few minutes then each said a prayer and goodnight to one another exactly at 7:30 P.M.

Ty began reading out loud from the Bible, and a short time later Caroline's eyes were closed. He made sure the candle was burning right; he had it sitting on top of a plate beside the bed on the rug.

Now it was time for him to call his Confidante and see how her night and day had gone. He dialed the number and said hello.

"Hello," she replied.

She asked all the same questions. "How's Caroline? Have you noticed anything different?" She would tell Ty how his writing had gone for the day. She never asked; she already knew. Ty didn't know how she knew, but she did. She was good. He was learning more about that every day. Nothing got by her; she knew what they were dealing with and that was for sure. She was spiritually blessed, strong, powerful, smart, faithful and compassionate. It was now simple to see that she was ready to see if Ty wanted to be healed—not be saved by her but healed. She also wanted to see if Ty would do anything to prove it. He had to show faith.

Ty wasn't getting a chance to do much talking these past few nights on the phone. He was mostly listening or trying to ask a question. It just seemed like things were moving too quickly.

She asked Ty a second time how he was feeling. Right away, he felt something was about to happen.

"What now?" he asked.

"Things aren't looking good for you right now because of your religious status," she said.

"So? Am I going to die tonight?" he replied sarcastically.

"That would be up to you whether or not you can stay up all night," she responded.

He could not fall asleep at all tonight, she told him. The young spirit was going to try and take Ty by fire this night.

Ty jumped up and went to the kitchen to make sure everything was turned off. He never did turn on the pilot light to the heater so that couldn't be a problem. The candle was safely burning next to the bed, but Ty was starting to panic. He asked all kinds of questions, over and over—was she sure?

"That's what the church sees happening tonight." She was speaking on behalf of the help she was getting from the church, she said.

Ty was so angry it did not matter whether he told her about his experiences at the beach; she probably already knew, he mumbled to himself.

"Ok! If I fall fast asleep tonight, Caroline and I are going to burn to death, is that right?" he asked.

She told him what she saw and she told him what he was supposed to do.

Ty was looking around the room. So how in hell was this going to happen, he wondered?

"Write all night and pray and keep your eyes open. Do you understand?" she commanded.

She was firm with every word of advice. She explained that she had to get back to the church as it was all she could think about. She was going to be up all night to help, praying and working on his problem in her church. "Show faith and the will to live, and be sure to call me before you get Caroline up for school," she said.

Ty told her that he loved her, and thanked her before hanging up the phone. He had nine hours to go until six o'clock A.M.

Chapter 12

Ty lay back against the pillow and considered all he had to write about. And so he started writing, only to find himself paralyzed with fear. His heart was beating wildly. Ty was being tested and to make matters worse, he had to chronicle the events that had already taken place at the old house. Ty would have to relive the spectral fire that had raged through the house on Newton Street, as well as Joseph's supernatural rape of Jackie. He was mixed up with too many bad memories running through his head.

Ty even started doubting some things he had been told by his Confidante. He was exhausted and losing it. It was now two o'clock and he was doing the best he could with the writing while fighting to stay awake. His brain was working overtime, his lack of sleep casting a shadow of uncertainty over the entire enterprise.

He checked the candle alongside the bed with compulsive regularity to be sure it wasn't in danger of setting the rug on fire. He had secured it in such a way that there was no possibility of it falling or igniting anything. It was completely out of the way of everything.

Ty tried listening to his own voice as he started dozing off telling himself what not to do. Then all of a sudden, he snapped out of this cloud of doubt and confusion as he remembered one conversation, the one when he first called the Confidante. She had told him she'd been waiting for his call. Somehow that did it. Those words got him back online. He knew that this night had to be real.

He promised himself he was not going to die tonight, and then he fell asleep. It took a while before his eyes opened and he smelled smoke. The smoke was burning his eyes. The note pad he was holding was aflame.

Ty immediately started hitting the pad to put the fire out. It had burned through two pages clearly and was starting to cook the third. Shocked awake by a surge of adrenaline, Ty was panting when he looked down at the candle at bedside to make sure it was still secure. The wax from the candle had made its way to the carpet, through the plate. It did not overrun the plate—it had gone directly through the plate and onto the carpet. He didn't know how that happened, but he did know the boy spirit was trying to kill them. He instantly checked on Caroline. She was asleep. Tears came to Ty's eyes once he absorbed all that had just taken place. He became angry and said out loud: "Goddammit, what in the blue hell is going on in my life and in the world?" He put the candle out.

It was now about four o'clock in the morning. He didn't even attempt to figure out how the notebook paper had started to burn. Feeling suddenly victorious, Ty was up talking trash, knowing the evil spirit had been unsuccessful in his attack by fire.

Six o'clock came and Ty had his Confidante's phone ringing off the hook. There were angry tears gathered under his eyes, but no tear ran down his face. There was no self-pity in him. "That no good spook boy thinks he's going to win because he led me down a dead end road for so long and I followed him. Now he's trying to kill me," Ty decided. He was a lost soul in the land of the living, preaching to his Confidante whether he made sense or not. Ty's nerves were worn down and he actually got a little huffy on the phone.

His Confidante listened as he went off at fifty miles a minute, letting him get it all out. When he was finished, she spoke: "Okay, it seems that young Joseph showed up after all. What happened?" she asked.

"I'm fed up with this! Why me?" he demanded.

"You asked that same question once before but I will answer it again," she said patiently. She explained that the Higher Power had chosen Ty and that he must demonstrate his faith and write it all down. "Remember, when it is all said and done, and the Higher Power has come, you will be on the Higher Power's right-hand side and all will see that you are blessed," she told him, as if it were the most ordinary thing in the world.

It was way too much for Ty to comprehend at this point, however. He had almost been burned alive. "Shit! Is this some kind of a gut check—or a reality check?" he mumbled.

"Well get a hold of whatever it is you want to call it because I have another package that the church is putting together for you, and I will let you know when I am going to send it," the Confidante went on. "I am going to need some more help because other things are going to happen."

"It's getting late!" Ty declared abruptly, showing real attitude. "I have got to get Caroline up and get her fed and prepared for school." he said, almost pleading.

"Okay. But call back. There is something I am going to need from you right away," she said as they said their good-byes.

After he hung up the phone, Ty lay still for a moment. He always felt good in the daylight, and he guessed that things were cool. His Confidante would have told him if there was danger, he thought. But then he had hung up before she finished. It was getting hard to think on his own.

He got Caroline up. She said she had slept well and was very happy and hungry. Ty got her ready and she looked so pretty. They were sitting at the table and she had a look of concern on her face.

"How did the writing go last night, Dad?" she asked.

"It went well. I'll be writing some more today while you're in school," he assured her.

On the way out the door, Ty told Caroline not to worry. "It's Friday and in two more days we get to go and pray with the Higher Power in church." That made her happy when he talked about going to church.

As he drove away from the school grounds Ty thought he would go crazy if he were ever to lose her to any of this madness surrounding them. Also, for just a minute, Ty thought he'd sensed that she was aware of the incident he'd had with the burning of the note pad. Maybe she wasn't asleep. And what more did his Confidante want from him, he asked himself. He kept up the same ongoing conversation with himself he had conducted ever since this situation began.

Speaking of conversations, it was time for Ty to hurry back to the apartment and learn what the Confidante needed from him next. It turned out that she wanted a picture of his family. She wanted to know what they looked like, and what condition their souls were in.

Ty later sent her a photo of himself, Jackie and Caroline together; it had been taken the previous Halloween and was their most recent picture taken together.

Ty and the Confidante spoke more about the previous night's ordeal. Ty was pleased to know that his Confidante, with her keen sense of anticipation, was able to handle his pretending not to be frightened out of his skin while learning the facts, and realizing the reality of the evil spirit. He couldn't thank her enough during this conversation.

She lifted his spirits by telling him that it was team work, but to hold on to all the thanks because it was far from over. That young spirit Joseph was making devastating plans and making them fast. She wanted Caroline and Ty to get out of town for a couple of weeks.

Ty knew she was serious so he didn't ask much. He said that he would start making plans for the end of May, as that would be the start of summer break.

She insisted that it was a must that he and Caroline isolate themselves as much as possible.

"What about this weekend?" Ty asked. "What is going to happen this weekend? I need to know if things are coming down on us." He couldn't hold the questions back any longer. "Do we need to leave now? I know just the place to go." The Confidante said that they were safe for this weekend as there would be good spirits and angels around them through the nights, and they would sleep well. There would be no chance of wrongdoing and it was going to be a busy weekend for everyone.

Jackie was going to be busy with her mom and other engagements that she had already made during the week. The Confidante's instructions were clear. "You need to see to your candles being lit, and pray, and bed down each night by eight o'clock for the rest of the weekend. Call me as soon as you get out of church on Sunday. I am going to be in prayer until then. You are not to worry. You are to show your strength, and strong faith and I will be waiting to hear from you!"

Ty felt lonely the instant he hung up the phone, separated from all the good that once stood out in him. Ty couldn't stand just sitting, wallowing in self-pity, and feeling the shame growing in his thoughts. All it did was make him angry and cause him to have hateful thoughts about people who were supposed to be family and friends. He didn't like the way that evil had entered into his family's life this way, but he knew what would bring him out of this pitiful and shameful state—the blessing of the Higher Power.

It was time to pick Caroline up from school and make her feel very much wanted.

They got something to eat at McDonald's, and when they got back to the apartment, he made sure that everything went smoothly. He let her go out to play for a while.

Ty kept everything at the apartment wide open, the doors and windows, so lots of light and air could circulate, and it made everything seem so alive and fresh. It also kept him from feeling so alone. He spent the time preparing dinner while Caroline played, and picked out a movie for after dinner which would run them close to bedtime. Passing time was important because it was going to be a long weekend without being able to talk to his Confidante.

Friday night went fine. Saturday night was much the same except they prepared for church on Sunday morning. Ty and Caroline slept well both nights and were feeling fine.

Ty was a little anxious on Sunday morning. He wanted to get to church as soon as possible, so he could get a seat toward the front. Church was full this morning, as they had two guest speakers from Oakland giving the sermon, which was excellent.

Ty never took an eye off the speakers. They spoke so clearly, it was as if the message was meant for him directly. The guest speakers and Ty kept eye contact throughout the entire service. One of them gave Ty the feeling that he knew something about him—or perhaps he knew everything. It was very strange.

As church neared its end and the song of invitation was being sung, a young man came forward to be baptized. As he went into the back room to prepare himself, the church grew louder, the voices standing out and well heard. The whole church was involved and it was all quite beautiful. The Higher Power was there. Ty could tell and began to feel very nervous. His body felt something he could not make out. The verse of the song was being repeated over and over, calling all sinners to come home.

Ty was in an anticipatory mood. What was keeping him in his seat he didn't know, beside the fact that he was frightened by the intensity building around him. Finally the curtain opened and the baptism was ready to begin. The singing stopped.

Ty's heart stopped pounding and returned to normal. After the baptism everyone got up and started for the door. It was potluck Sunday where everyone stayed over and helped themselves to a nice lunch.

Ty remembered standing in an aisle talking to one of the ladies his family knew well, and he remembered the lady remarked on how the church just kept on singing. "I thought for sure you were going to go forth," she said.

Ty told her that he really did want to come forth, but he wanted more family members to be there to witness his baptism. Ty added that he was going out of town, and wanted to be baptized when he got back, and felt good about that. They hugged each other and celebrated. Ty went on to say that he couldn't stay for lunch, having things to do. He looked around but didn't see where Caroline had gone off.

He started walking toward the door to go look for her so they could leave. When he got to the door, the guest speakers were still talking to some of the departing members of the congregation that were leaving, shaking their hands and thanking them for coming. Ty stood in line waiting his turn to meet them.

As he reached out to shake one's hand and introduce himself, the other guest speaker asked: "Are you the one who has been in touch with the Higher Power? Where are you going?"

He didn't really know how to respond, but the minister was persistent on the subject. Ty was stunned because he had never seen or heard of this man in his life.

"Why didn't you come forth?" the minister asked.

"Well, I plan to be baptized when I get back from a trip in a few weeks, and I wanted my family members to attend, and to be a part of this," Ty tried to explain.

"What do you mean in a few weeks?" the minister demanded. "You want your family members to witness your baptism? It doesn't work like that. It's not about family members being here, and in a few weeks it could be too late. I came all the way down from Oakland to baptize you today. It is your day. I am not going to let you leave this church until I do. If it is necessary, I am willing to follow you home," he said quite seriously.

Ty was staring at both of them and realized after several seconds that these ministers were set in their purpose. So he simply stopped trying to make excuses, because nothing but gibberish was coming out of his mouth anyway.

Ty looked around and the pastor of the church was now standing next to him, speaking: "All I can tell you and hope it makes you feel at ease, is that the Higher Power is waiting for you, and now would be the right time to wash your sins away and be born again in the name of our Father, the Son, and the Holy Spirit." This was followed by a rousing: "Amen." Next thing Ty knew he was being marched down the aisle to the back of the church.

When he passed through the door, he looked back into the church and saw that it was empty. Both guest speakers and the pastor of the church were in the back with him. Ty was asked a question about his belief in the Higher Power. While he answered the question, he changed into his baptismal garb, pulling things out of each pocket. He had a prayer book in one and a stone and rosary in the others. Ty was armed with it all.

There was so much he wanted to say, but he was tongue-tied, twisted and worse. He knew that he was not supposed to say much to anyone. So, he just kept quiet, but not very still. The nerves in his body shook to the bone.

The minister baptizing Ty spoke: "I know you have a lot you wanted to say and talk about, but now isn't the time. Your time is coming and you will be able to help so many with what you will have to say." Then, suddenly, Ty heard the sound of voices— rejoicing and singing—coming from the church. It grew louder and louder as they prepared for the baptism.

Ty was standing in the water, very nervous. His heart went back to beating like a drum. When the curtain opened, he looked out into the church and it was packed to the rafters. "Where did all these people come from?" he wondered. It looked like there were more people now than there had been when the sermon was delivered.

Caroline was sitting right in the front row.

Ty remembered going under the water and how fresh and overwhelmed and happy he felt when he emerged. He could not stop smiling. Ty was feeling strong. He had been baptized! He was now a member of The Church of Christ. He was buried with the Higher Power in baptism on the 18th day of May 1997 at the Church of Christ in Seaside, California. Now it was time to honor the way he felt about being a child of the Higher Power.

Ty was ready to brag in front of the evil spirit himself, but didn't because temptations from evil were going to lurk around him on all corners now. All he'd ever heard was that it gets tougher than ever being a son of the Higher Power. He was truly ready to leave town now. He felt he would have a better chance at resisting evil now because he wouldn't be around anyone for long, and all he would be doing is reading the Bible, and writing every day, all day. He was looking to be challenged, so he could show off this new strength he had encountered.

Ty hugged and shook everyone's hand and stayed behind for a while after the baptism and asked everyone to pray for him and Caroline as they were leaving town the following Friday. Once more, he hugged and held both ministers from Oakland, and thanked them so much for coming to the Church of Christ and bringing such a sermon that he would never forget. He was also grateful for the new light of life, and a chance to cherish that eternal salvation he looked forward to.

The minister said, "Share your story and pass the good word to the next one, and we shall meet again."

"Amen, I will," Ty replied. He and Caroline made it to their car and drove off safely. As they continued up the street from the church, Ty hollered out, "Yes!"

"Dad, I'm so proud of you," Caroline said and smiled.

"Thank you, Caroline. This is a brand-new start for me and it is not going to be easy. Being baptized gives me a whole new out look on life," Ty replied.

When they got back to the apartment, she gave Ty a hug and agreed to finish talking about the baptism in bed that night. For the rest of the day he let her play outside.

Ty once again left everything open, and enjoyed the fresh feeling in the apartment. He told Caroline to check back with him regularly so he would know that everything was okay.

Ty sat down and calmed himself enough to dial his Confidante's phone number. It was time to share his good news with her. He knew she would be happy for him. The phone rang three times, four and then came that voice in Ty's time of need. It was the voice that he wanted to hear and the person he wanted to speak with.

"Hello there," Ty said.

"Hi. How was church this morning?" She knew he had gotten home a little late. "Is everything all right?" she asked.

Ty explained that everything was fine, and church had been very good to him. He had stayed after for a while, there was a potluck lunch and he had a little to eat and so did Caroline. He told her proudly that he was baptized today, and explained that the way it all took place was strange but wonderful. He felt so good about it, and went on to explain how it all came about and who had baptized him. She was very happy of course just as he thought she would be.

"I am so glad that everything went as scheduled," she said.

That kind of puzzled Ty. "You sounded as if you knew ahead of time that I was going to be baptized on this day."

"Well, I did. I didn't want to force anything, so you would be yourself, and it would have no effect on your behavior. This way everything happened naturally," she explained.

"Naturally," Ty replied.

She explained that on a Catholic calendar Ty's reborn day had already been scheduled, and it was meant to be. As always, while talking with her, he had learned to expect the unexpected. Some things were a little more shocking than others though. It just gave him more faith in her and more faith in the Higher Power, and it let him know that his life had a meaning, and there was a purpose for all of this taking place.

Ty's biggest problem was still fear. Living up to all of this was frightening for him. Whether it was good or bad, it was about spiritual living. The Higher Power wanted him to walk and talk in the Higher Power's footsteps and those are some big footsteps to walk in. Ty wanted to walk that walk real bad and no matter what it took he was determined to try.

After hearing what the Confidante knew already, Ty thought it was best that he didn't know what was on the fate calendar for that day. He had enough pressure on himself as it was. He talked more about the morning and the day, and then they started planning for their trip, and what all he had to do. Ty was to make all of the reservations to leave on Friday morning. They were going to Yuma, Arizona—dry land; a place out of the way. Ty knew a couple there—Frank and Lucy Winston and their two girls, April and Leslie, who were about the same age as Caroline. The Winstons would be the only people they would associate with when they got there. Ty was planning on asking them to pick up him and Caroline at the airport.

Then he looked up at the front door and saw Jackie stalking down the walkway toward the apartment. He immediately told his Confidante that he would call back because Jackie was there.

Ty hung the phone up quickly, and got up and met Jackie at the door. She looked really fine and he told her so. It was a surprise to see her. They were both a little quiet though. Before Ty started telling her about his day, he asked about hers.

First, she told him that she had been to church and had spent a good part of the afternoon with her mother on their usual Sunday outing. She talked about some other things she did and how she was ready to see Caroline.

Ty played his day down a little so he wouldn't get hurt. He had to be careful, since he really didn't know how she would react—or which Jackie was standing in front of him, especially since he had been giving her the cold shoulder. To top it off, Ty never told Jackie he and Caroline were planning on leaving in five days for a couple of weeks without her. He was going to be really pushing it if he expected Jackie to jump for joy. Anyway, he told her everything and she responded quietly, showing no feelings, and becoming very cold. She changed the subject by asking where Caroline was.

Ty went and got her. Jackie only remained behind a few more minutes. She got some hugs and kisses from Caroline and then said she had to go.

Caroline was hurt. She wanted to do something with her mom. Ty felt the change and the tension building and his spirits were changing for the worse. But he was trying to keep everything positive. All of a sudden Jackie started backing down the walkway. Caroline and Ty both felt she didn't want to be there.

Ty tried walking out to the car with her, but could barely keep up. She got in her car and left. Ty was lost for words. He tried to smile, but wanted to cry.

He then turned around real fast and jogged back to the apartment. Caroline had already gone back to playing with some local kids.

Ty closed the door and sat down on the bean bag. Getting comfortable, he began thinking. He couldn't blame anybody for what was taking place in his life. He knew there were two sides to this problem. Fixing one side wasn't going to be enough. He really needed and wanted to get away from Jackie and everything else around him and right then! It really hurt him that Caroline didn't get to spend the time with her mom as she should have.

There was a lot of anger coming out of Ty, and he would always try to use that anger to build up a wall against the hurting, and gain the strength he needed daily.

Ty grabbed the phone and called his Confidante back to tell her what had transpired. She told him not to worry because there was nothing Ty could do to change Jackie's reaction to his transformation and the new direction he had taken.

"Do not change the way you are living at the apartment just to stay on the safe side for the rest of the week. Do not try to fix anything that happened today as far as what took place with Jackie. It's done! Don't call her, and if she calls tonight keep the conversation short. Comfort Caroline, write, and get some rest because you are going to need it," she promised.

Ty loved his Confidante and he told her so.

"Good-bye," Ty said.

"Good-bye," she answered.

Ty bounced up off that bean bag the best he could and got back on his routine. He prepared for dinner, and got Caroline's school clothes ready for the next morning.

When Caroline checked in, she had a couple more hours of daylight left. Ty figured he would let her play a little while longer as it gave him a chance to unwind and it kept her happy.

Caroline finally did come in and went right into her normal routine as well. She ate well, and after dinner got cleaned up and hopped into bed, where she started talking about the Higher Power, while Ty got the dishes put away and cleaned up.

She asked quite a few questions before saying a nice prayer, and both of them fell fast asleep. The next day came quickly.

Caroline went to school. Ty was nervous as usual before receiving any news from the Confidante. Soon the phone rang and he quickly answered it.

"Well, how did you and Caroline sleep last night?" his Confidante asked.

"Please, my nerves are about to wear me out this morning. Tell me that I have no worries," Ty pleaded.

"First the package," she said sternly. "It will be there tomorrow morning at ten o'clock."

She wanted Ty to listen carefully before he asked any more questions. "The package is for the old house. You are going to take the contents in the package to that house, and do as I tell you. You are to call as soon as you get this package. I will go over every item with you and explain what to do with each one, just as we did with the other packages. Now, do you have a key to get in the old house?" she asked.

"I know where Jackie kept a key for the landlord so he could get in. I can use that one," Ty said.

"That's good," she said. "You cannot let anyone know about this and you are going to need to use Jackie's car when you go there tomorrow. That's very important," she stressed.

She knew how much Ty worried about Jackie living in that house. So Jackie was going to need help and some protection while Ty was out of town. It would help him as well, since he would be able to concentrate on his work.

"Now, about your worrying, you have a lot to think about. You should only worry if you don't do as you have been chosen to do. Let's not use the word 'worry' so much. Having faith is the key to what has to be done right now. Have a positive day and get some writing in. Keep those candles going and get some rest tonight. Don't forget, ten o'clock tomorrow I will be waiting to hear from you. Good-bye," she said.

"Bye."

The phone conversation was over and Ty sat holding the phone speechless.

"Shit! I don't want tomorrow to come," he said to himself.

Ty just sat there and tried to get some writing in but couldn't stop thinking about that awful house he had to re-enter the next day.

He didn't know how he was supposed to get any rest tonight, so he just sat and day dreamed.

Time flew by and before he knew it Caroline was home. Ty really didn't remember going and getting her from school. Bedtime came fast and they fell asleep right away. When Ty woke up, he was drained.

He got up and fixed a good breakfast for Caroline and himself. With a full stomach, he lay back down after taking Caroline to school and fell back asleep until a knock on the door woke him up. He jumped up, sure that the package had arrived. It had.

Ty signed for it and then closed the door and sat down. He started brainstorming and a few moments passed, after which he picked up the phone and started trying to prepare himself for this dreadful morning and the true test of courage. He and his Confidante got right down to business.

Ty opened the package and pulled out each item one by one, and set it all on the table.

He took the piece of paper out last. The list of things was on it, including garlic, a bottle of holy water, a large cross, and a card with a picture on one side and a prayer on the other.

The Confidante finished giving Ty the details, and told him to give her a call when he got back. The first thing he had to do was to make sure Jackie was not leaving work early for lunch.

Ty called her after hanging up the phone with his Confidante, and made up a light conversation with her. Jackie said the girls all brought their lunch today. She normally went home for lunch. Okay so far. The phone call went well.

Ty drove to her work and his first attempt to trade cars failed. One of Jackie's co-workers came out to her car and Ty had to dodge her driving around the parking lot one more time.

No sooner had he gotten into her car than he felt the company. He pretended as if he did not recognize it. As he got closer to the old house, Ty's fear escalated. He started going over all that he had to do in such a little time. Ty only had five minutes to get in and out and away from that house or all hell was going to break loose.

When he pulled up in front of the house on Newton St., Ty tried not to look at it, but couldn't help notice that it looked ten times older than it had the last time he was there. Actually he was trying to get out of the damn car before it even stopped. He knew the second he pulled up in front of that house that his five minutes had started.

Ty parked the car and brought out a hammer and nails, along with all the other required objects. The Confidante wanted him to put the garlic in front of the house by the entrance just beneath the surface.

Ty bent down and came face to face with the air vent that led under the house. He tried to look the other way but caught the sound and whiff of fetid breath that caused him to drop his nails and garlic onto the dirt. Aware of the time ticking away, he used the claw of the hammer to dig the hole by the front door, and then scooted in the garlic and covered it. With the foul air becoming worse he covered his nose and mouth and began frantically pushing through the dirt to find the nails.

Ty came to his feet blowing the dirt off the nails and putting them in his mouth, preparing for his next move—going inside. It was very difficult for him to climb the few steps to the front door. They creaked as he stepped on each one. Forgetting the placement of the key for a split second and thinking he had brought the key with him, Ty reached into his pocket and felt something he knew he didn't put there. The experience caused Ty to quickly inhale while freeing his hand, pulling the inside of his pants pocket out and almost swallowing a nail. The key was where he expected it to be, under the mat.

Ty opened the door and the company that he had felt in her car on the ride over to the old house grew closer as he stood in the doorway. He was trying to recover as his ears were ringing after coughing so. He was sweating profusely, terrified as he stood there, looking inside this house. His ears ringing made it sound like low wicked laughter coming from inside the house. He could not stand in the doorway much longer because time was running out.

The first thing he did once he got inside was to sprinkle the holy water in every corner of the house. Every step he took the floors creaked, and he could hear the wakening of something so large it seemed to bend the floor boards, walls and ceiling. Whatever it was got Ty moving a little faster, keeping a close eye on his watch. The toughest part for Ty was not knowing what was in each section of the house before entering it. By now there was so much saliva built up in Ty's mouth from holding the nails that it began seeping out the sides and he was breathing through his nose, blowing like a buffalo, intensifying his every move. He also kept one eye on the front door. The time was important, but so was the front door. He kept it on his mind, in case he had to make a sudden exit. He decided he would exit the way he came in—through the front door. He was not only scared, but he was serious. He drenched the hide-a-bed with holy water, and the bed shook. Ty quickly held the card with the prayer out at the bed, hesitating to move for a few seconds, then placed the card inside the china cabinet.

He then got something to stand on as it wasn't easy to place the cross up high in the area where Jackie slept. Ty was shaking as he dropped one nail from his mouth to the ground, but took another out and hammered it in place and put the arrangement she had there over the cross. No one would know that the cross was there except those spirits. The next time that young Joseph tried to go forth with his obsession in completing the takeover of Jackie's soul, he will have this cross to deal with. Ty knew from experience the evil spirits didn't like this kind of heat.

He had seen it with his own eyes, and being back in this real live haunted house putting his life in a deadly situation, he did not like it. The undulating house was becoming more unsettled. Ty was trying not to imagine what something would look like if it popped out from around a corner.

He was very scared, and was trying not to show it. Even though he was prepared for his nervous mistakes, Ty still had to be careful about rushing. He had to be sure how much holy water he was putting in each corner of the house, as he couldn't afford to run out. He had to have enough to go all the way around the shed, barn, and the outside of the house. It was intense. He had to watch every move he made.

There was a cross around his neck, beads and all showing. The special rock he had received was in his pocket. Ty had a lot going for him and being baptized really made him feel invincible. Still, he would rather have been invisible for this situation.

He left walking backwards, commando-style, out of the house. He put the key back in its hiding place and started spreading the holy water around the house and shed. Afterwards, he hustled into the car, started it up and sped off. The bad company never did leave his side.

In the car his bad company was making its presence known by stepping up the intensity level. Ty took off the cross he was wearing and tossed it over his shoulder so it was quite visible behind him. He managed to reach into his pants pocket slowly, and pulled out the special rock and held it tight.

He then began repeating the Higher Power prayer over and over, and tried to keep from driving so erratically! He had one more job that had to be done once he got back to the parking lot where Jackie worked.

He parked the car but before he got out, he went into a rage, forgetting where he was for the moment. He brought out the holy water that he had saved and started splashing it everywhere.

At the parking lot at Jackie's work, Ty got out of her car and hurried to his own vehicle. He retrieved a cross, and tossed it on the floorboard in the back seat of Jackie's car. It put the fear of the Higher Power into those evil spirits, and they hurried like gangbusters getting out of that car.

Ty not only heard them, but he also saw them. He knew things would be a little uneasy for the rest of the day, but he didn't care because at the end of the week he and Caroline were leaving. He kept that in mind the entire time.

He got into his car, returned to the apartment and called his Confidante to let her know he was still alive and his job was done.

She was pleased. She reminded him that Jackie's mind was already being controlled by the young evil spirit. She shared the picture of Ty's family, and it proved to her and to the eye of her church that the young spirit had made several attempts on Caroline, and would continue.

"The extent of your life will be based upon the extent of your faith. Now here's what you have to do to prepare yourself for company in the worst way on your little vacation," she said.

Ty interrupted abruptly, saying; "I thought I was leaving this shit all behind!"

"Get a hold of yourself! Yes, there are some things you can leave behind and there are other things that will always be there, and now it a good time to talk and prepare for these things. Let's go back in time. You had left yourself open for so long, this young evil spirit thinks it is just a matter of time before he destroys you," she explained.

Ty was back sweating again.

"What am I supposed to do? What am I going to do? he asked.

"Counter, stall, get this young evil spirit one on one. This is the purpose of your trip, getting away from all of your temptations. It's in his favor here.

"They are going to follow you, watching your every move, trying very hard for Caroline. Remember, she is the key to his success, or so he thinks. This is why you must limit your visitation with your friends in Arizona. The fewer conversations you have with anyone will be in your favor because you don't know what seed has been planted to grow around you or to distract you from your business at hand," she said. "Understood?" she asked.

Ty told her that he totally understood her. Now he just needed to stay calm on the plane ride. Ty did not like to fly.

His Confidante told him the plane would be safe and that she would see to it.

Her faith and power and her spiritual connection with the Higher Power was of a degree Ty wished someday to share. They spent all morning and some of the afternoon on the phone until it was time again to pick up Caroline from school.

This routine continued as it had except Ty didn't sleep well the rest of the week. Caroline on the other hand was excited about going on an airplane, and had slept like a baby each night. Time went by very quickly.

Chapter 13

They took a taxi to the airport where Ty unloaded the cab, paid the driver and checked in. He had all of his instructions for their stay in Arizona in hand and was ready to board the plane. Everyone was very nice. Caroline was the main attraction and even got herself a pair of wings while Ty scored the window seat.

Ty took one look out that window and his eyes started seeing things, and his mind started to wander. He began to sweat and become nervous, as if he was under attack by something that was trying to drive him right out of his seat. Ty suddenly felt certain that there was going to be a problem with the plane.

As each passenger entered the plane and passed by his seat, Ty would stare and try to analyze them. He felt himself losing control, so he closed his eyes and kept them closed until his heart stopped racing.

He took a deep breath and tried to focus on the conversation he had had with his Confidante at the beginning of week.

When he opened his eyes, a stewardess asked if everything was all right, and if he needed a soft drink.

"Please," he responded.

Caroline asked for a drink as well. The stewardess waited until the plane took off and then brought them both something to drink.

Ty sipped at his beverage and asked himself: "What happened to all your faith?" It was silly for him to forget the gameplan so soon. As always, when he felt he'd gotten a handle on things, he would start with the lecture, but this time he tried not to make it so obvious. He kept it to himself and pondered quietly.

The flight wasn't long but regardless of Ty's frequent military travel all over the world, he simply did not like to fly. It was already time to put up the trays and prepare to land. So much for trying to stay calm. Ty didn't care much for the landing part either.

Frank and Lucy Winston and their girls were already at the airport arrivals area waiting for Ty and Caroline.

Leslie and April were excited to see Caroline and everyone started talking at the same time.

Ty had this feeling that Caroline was trying to forget about the conversation they'd had about this trip. He was hoping he wouldn't have a hard time separating the girls, as his Confidante had instructed.

The ride back to the Winston's house was nerve racking with everyone suggesting what they should do. Ty finally had to put an end to it. He told them that Caroline would stay with them before they took the trip to the city. April's birthday had passed, but she was promised a trip to Phoenix, where a huge water park awaited.

Ty told Caroline that they would go along as long as they handled their business first. Ty got everyone in agreement. While at Frank and Lucy's house, he made reservations for him and Caroline to stay at the Shilo Inn, located in the nicest area in town. It had everything and there would be no need to leave the Inn other than for Ty to do his banking. He and Caroline were set.

Ty had the Winstons drive them over to the Shilo Inn. Of course the girls wanted to swim in the pool once they pulled up in front of the luxurious motel.

Ty checked himself and Caroline into their room. While the girls wandered all over, the three adults went on up to the room. Ty didn't care for the girls running around the Inn, but there wasn't much he could do about it.

The room had a great view of the pool, and Ty could see the temptation everywhere. It was growing late and Ty assumed Frank and Lucy had their own agenda for the weekend. Plus, their girls were still in school. That was good, since it kept Caroline from asking if Leslie and April could come over or if she could visit their house.

Once the girls came inside from the pool area, they rode the elevator up to see the room.

Ty really needed to make a phone call as his Confidante was waiting and he desperately needed some privacy. He started clock watching but his guests finally left and he started preparing the room just as they had done back at the apartment.

Ty blessed the room with holy water in every corner and then made himself comfortable while Caroline ate and watched television. He lay back for a couple minutes and then called his Confidante.

The first thing she asked was: "Are you in your room?"

"Yes," he responded.

She wanted to know every detail about the Inn. She sounded so delighted, Ty thought she was leaving New Jersey and meeting him here. As it turned out, however, this was the perfect place to draw those evil spirits to something of luxury, pleasure, things that were expensive and very materialistic.

By no means was Ty looking forward to their company, but he was mentally prepared and honestly ready to get to the bottom of this as well. His Confidante was going back over his agenda, as it was finally starting to dawn on Ty why he was really here.

It was to give her a chance to learn more about the growing strength of young Joseph, and how much time Ty had before the spirit attempted a fatal strike. Here at the Inn, Ty and Caroline were pretty much isolated.

Ty was not going to sin in any way, but he was sure the evil spirit felt it was worth the wait to see if he would be tempted by the women that would be working out at the gym or lounging by the pool. Some days were harder than others, but the support from his Confidante every morning and night kept Ty straight. When he wasn't on the phone with her, Ty would be deep into writing his story next to the place he had already discovered was most effective—by water and in this case it was the pool, where he would react to some of the strange things he felt.

As the days and nights came and went, Ty started feeling more pressure. One day while he wrote vigorously at poolside, the sun burning down and the sweat pouring off him, he paused and dove into the pool.

Ty came up out of the water and for the first time noticed something in the direction of his room. It was shocking; he tried to pinpoint their exact room without being obvious, and then prayed that what he saw was not emanating from their room. But of course it was.

Ty got out of the pool trying to play off this disturbing situation, as the shock made its impact throughout his neuromuscular system in an attempt to shut him down. He reached for a towel and put it over his head, then sat down and peered out at Caroline. She was having a ball all by herself. By the time each day ended she would be water-logged and starving. After she ate and cleaned up, five minutes into her television programs she would fall fast asleep. Since there was no need for a change, Ty left her alone and didn't let her feel the changes in his demeanor.

In the meantime, he was playing peek-a-boo through the towel, trying to see if that large darkness he had glimpsed above their room was still there. It was.

The evil spirit and his company were making it known that they had found their way to the Inn and were rampaging in Ty's room. They were moving around in a frantic manner, unable to get comfortable in this room. Ty knew he could count on some kind of reaction and he was getting it.

He had a quick thought. Each time he left the room in the morning he took down all the crosses on the windows and doors and put them in the drawers and closet, out of sight of the maids. So, if evil spirits were trying to find some darkness, it was going to be difficult for them. The heat in that room also had to be unbearable for them.

Ty didn't let this interruption change anything in his program for the day. He just kept writing, and stopped looking at the room. He did not want anything or anyone to catch him feeling or looking the least bit worried. He knew how important it was for him to write, to get all the things that took place in the past down on paper while his Confidante had her candle light going. That's how their souls and spirits stayed connected.

Ty kept reminding himself of that and of how much he needed her help and those thoughts kept him focused on his writing. It was still difficult to focus, wondering what was going on with those spirits in his room. Ty had no intentions of finding out any time soon. He was just going to have to wait and find out later. Ty needed to make a bank run and decided to go later that afternoon. He had already asked Frank to give him a ride there and back, now all he had to do was call Frank. When the time came to go, Ty used the phone in the lobby to make his call.

Frank showed up with the whole family and as soon as Ty and Caroline got into the car the girls started talking all at once, the whole way to the bank. After the bank run, Ty bought the girls some McDonald's, remaining uptight the whole time, but remaining stoic. All he wanted to do was get back to the hotel and be by himself. They finally made it.

Frank dropped Ty and Caroline at the front entrance. They went in and Ty made a payment on the room for the next few days.

Ty thought hard taking the elevator up to their room, while Caroline couldn't wait to get there to eat her food. Ty kept it all together from the minute they entered the room, he remained calm. After Caroline finished her food she got in the bath tub and Ty replaced the crosses.

It soon got dark and Ty didn't have a clue as to what to expect. There was no sign of the spirits. He felt good about everything that had gone on so far other than the spook sighting earlier, so he kept tight to the game plan.

Ty cleaned up after Caroline and they got in bed. Ty lay with her until she fell asleep then got into the other bed and made some phone calls. First, he called room service and ordered a glass of red wine to help him relax. After that, he called his Confidante and told her all about what he saw and what he did.

She questioned Ty extensively about a few things, such as the trip to the bank. She asked him how much money he withdrew from the bank.

"On Sundays the banks are closed, so I used my ATM and could only get a few hundred dollars out," he explained. But she was concerned about the amount of money he kept around. She advised him not to keep large bills in his possession at any time, and his attention to any stranger was dangerous. He was not to let himself be consumed by anything or anybody. She made some comments about the trip Ty had planned with Frank, Lucy and the girls but other than that, she felt okay.

Ty promised her, "I will be careful." It was getting late and before Ty got off the phone, he asked about Jackie. "How is Jackie doing? I haven't talked to her in a week or better."

He and Caroline were starting to miss her, and Ty was becoming a little concerned.

The Confidante told him that Jackie was fine, and that he should send her a postcard. This was good for Ty to hear, and now he would sleep even better—especially after his glass of wine.

They said their goodnights to each another and Ty laid back and finished his wine. His mind began to wander, and his intuition on things grew stronger. He made sure everything was secured, and said a few prayers before falling fast asleep.

Ty got up early Monday morning, had some coffee and watched the news on TV. He did not care to think about yesterday. He carried on the same as the previous week, made one more bank run and remained at the Inn until Thursday morning, when they checked out.

Ty and Caroline left the Shilo Inn and went over to the Winston's house where they stayed the night. The girls were really happy to see each other again. The Winstons didn't have a pool so the girls played in the water sprinklers, and kept pretty busy throughout the evening. Ty just sat around with Frank and Lucy and watched TV.

The plan was to get an early start for the city the next day, but it didn't turn out that way. Everything that could possibly happen to slow down the start of the trip did.

The truck that Frank was going to use to haul most everything broke down while Frank and Ty were out last minute shopping for the trip. The truck was fixed but it took a while. Things were starting to get pretty negative. That's when Ty started to be more cautious in everything he did.

It turned out, for instance, that there was another couple that was supposed to go along on the trip but didn't show up. Frank called and called until he finally caught up with them, and found out they had to work late and couldn't go. It was a four-hour drive to the city, and they needed to get on the road soon. Ty made sure all of his and Caroline's things were on the truck because they would be catching a flight back to California from Phoenix. Frank made reservations already so they didn't have to rush to get there even though it was growing late. Finally they were all packed and ready to take off.

Ty rode in the car with Lucy and the girls, while Frank followed in the truck. They were about half way into the trip before Ty became tired of the girls. His nerves were bad and things got worse as the sun went down.

Ty recognized that Lucy wasn't driving very well but didn't want to say anything to her just yet. Instead, he asked the girls to quiet down and kept a close eye on Lucy's driving. It did not seem to get any better as the sun set and when she pulled into the next gas station, Ty asked if he could take over the driving. Lucy was delighted and confessed that she could not see well at night.

Ty wondered when or if she was going to share that information.

Ty drove the rest of the way and everything went well. The hotel was right across the street from the water park, and there were plenty of places to eat. That made things a lot easier, but the rooms were quite a distance from the vehicles.

After checking in and then going back and forth unpacking the car and the truck, Ty was ready to relax the rest of night, but he needed to call his Confidante to let her know they made it and give her an update.

Unfortunately, it didn't look like he was going to get the privacy he wanted for a while because the girls were migrating back and forth from one room to the other. They wanted to swim, they wanted to do this and that; they were on the move.

Ty ended up having to wait a long while before calling her. He couldn't stay put in his room either, and didn't like the idea of Caroline being in the pool without any supervision. As he began looking around and checking out the hotel, he suddenly started becoming very uncomfortable with the place. He realized he was right in the middle of a big party. Name it, and it was happening at this hotel.

Frank and Lucy finally made it over to the pool area. Frank had already found a party going on and asked Ty if he wanted to go. Ty told them he would watch the girls for awhile, and join them later.

They agreed happily and left. A lot of time had passed, and by now it had grown much later. It was time for the girls to get out of the pool.

Caroline and Ty walked Leslie and April back toward their room, and then turned around and headed back to their room, which was set up like a studio. It had a little kitchen, along with a TV room and bedroom. Ty fixed Caroline a little snack which she ate and then fell fast asleep.

Ty was now almost able to think clearly. He got the holy water out of his bag and sprinkled it in every corner of the room and put up the crosses.

He tried to sit down and relax but could not. Something had him on edge. Maybe it was all the noise the people at the hotel were making. He finally made the phone call to his Confidante, but the conversation was cut short. He locked up everything and got into bed before midnight, where he lay thinking. The Confidante wasn't happy at all abut the place or the situation he was in. He couldn't sleep if he wanted to. The traffic passing by his room was so bad he didn't trust his senses; he thought perhaps the noises came from inside his room. He really couldn't tell because the air conditioner was grinding so loudly.

When morning came he was relieved, but this morning did not start out well. Things were not organized. Ty still had one more night to go, and he was definitely planning to be better prepared.

The girls couldn't make up their minds where to eat after seeing all the fast food restaurants the previous night. So, Ty left everyone in one room trying to decide, and went to a restaurant by himself.

He tried to get Caroline to come, but she just wanted to continue following April and Leslie. Except all the fast food places they walked to were closed.

Ty watched them from where he sat. They finally gave up on eating, and walked right past the store where he was sitting and didn't even see him. Then they headed for the water park.

Ty hurried and finished eating so he could catch up with them, which he soon did.

He knew Caroline was very hungry, and didn't make her feel any better about her situation by gloating over his hearty breakfast.

When they all got inside the park, the rest of the group found something to eat. Once that was over it was time to head on over to the water area where the slides sliced and looped through the sky.

The slides were way too much for Caroline, and there were some even Ty wouldn't dare ride. She wouldn't go on any slides with Ty so they pretty much stood around watching until Lucy tricked Caroline into going on one of the water slides. She told Caroline it was a small one.

It wasn't. After Caroline's terrifying ride down one of the largest slides in the park, she would not stop crying. Ty's day was practically ruined. The heat was unbearable, it was burning Caroline's skin and Ty was very upset with Lucy. He was ready to leave the park. Frank and his family had been to the park before and were very familiar with all of the slides. That was why Ty was upset. Lucy eventually told Caroline she was sorry and the child finally stopped crying.

Ty told them to go on and enjoy their day and he and Caroline would be fine. In the end, they went over to the very small slides where she could play safely. Ty watched and waded in the water for hours.

Caroline finally decided she wanted to leave, since she was hungry and thirsty. They were on their way out of the park and ran into Frank, Lucy and the girls, who had also decided it was time to go. They all left together and no one bothered bringing up Caroline's bad experience in the park, and it was completely forgotten.

Back at the hotel Ty and Caroline were invited to the Winston's room for pasta and rolls. Ty stayed on until Frank and some friends of his started drinking, and he immediately left. Caroline stayed on and went swimming with Lucy, April and Leslie.

When Ty got back to his room, things didn't feel right. It felt as if someone had been in his room besides housekeeping. He checked the room over and nothing was missing, but still something bothered him.

He felt a presence in the room. He sat down and tried to get it together. While he was sitting there, he noticed the ring on his finger was dull, which was kind of strange because he shined it constantly. As a matter of fact, he had just shined it before they went to the park. He had even gotten many comments about it.

He took it off and put it on the kitchen counter and went back and sat down. This time he turned on the TV and tried to forget about whatever it was that was bothering him. It didn't work, of course, and now Ty felt as if something was staring at him, seriously staring. He could feel the direction the stare was coming from and started looking right in that direction. He didn't see any dark shadows, but it was now becoming very tense in the room. Ty felt certain that he was going to be attacked. He didn't know whether to run or to defend himself—but from what? He sat up and prepared himself, and made sure that if anything was going to come at him, it would come face on. Nothing could surprise him from behind. More and more he started recognizing this situation here in this hotel from his past experiences, and it felt exactly the same.

Ty roamed the room with his eyes again and again, looking hard for any dark or shaded areas. He never forgot that was the way that an evil spirit would form itself through darkness. But there wasn't any darkness.

Once more he gave a sharp look from one side to the other and just as he was passing by his ring, on the kitchen counter Ty got this enormous sense of negativity radiating from it.

Ty jumped up and rushed at the piece of jewelry, showing no fear. He grabbed the ring and balled his hand into a fist with the ring held tight.

He then walked into the other room where he had put his briefcase and opened it, removing the velvet ring bag. He put the ring in side the bag and tied the strings up so tightly that nothing could get out. He then wrapped the ring bag up in paper and locked it in the briefcase.

Ty went back into the TV room, picked up the phone and called his Confidante right away. While he was waiting for the Confidante to answer the phone, he started brainstorming. Could this ring be evil? What about all the other jewelry and whatever else he had received through dubious deals?

The Confidante interrupted his thoughts when she answered the phone.

"Hello?"

"Yes!" Ty responded with a trace of desperation in his voice.

All at once he blurted out everything that he thought he had discovered in the past twenty minutes. She was trying to keep up with what he had to say, and he was so excited that she could hear his heart beating. Finally, she had to slow him to a halt.

"Where did you get that ring?" she asked.

"It was negatively related. I got it from a fellow who sold antique Indian souvenirs and that fellow stole it from his father. I locked the ring up in my briefcase. I also think the ring caused my notes to catch fire the night I was awakened by smoke. Remember the time I was to be careful of fire, and I was not supposed to fall asleep," he recalled.

"Of course I remember," she said.

"I was wearing that ring on that night and there was a possibility the reflection between the light and the ring, caused it to have a magnifying glass effect on my notebook. The lamp light sat right next to the bed," he told her.

It didn't matter what took place then or now, Ty only wanted to get up safely in the morning and fly home, and then gather up everything that he felt was not safe or righteous at home and send it to the Confidante, so she could set his mind at ease. He really meant this. He had so many things that he could not possibly tell what was evil and what was not.

His Confidante told him that he was definitely on the right track. Now, Ty was ready to leave this place.

He got off the phone to go get Caroline. It was bedtime for both of them and Caroline was tired from all her swimming. Ty told Lucy that he didn't feel well and turned in for the night. On his way back to his room Ty took one more good look at the hotel and mumbled to himself: "This is no place I would park my car overnight."

Ty and Caroline got inside the room and prepared quickly for bed. He checked everything out and made sure things were turned off and locked up, and then he got in bed and practically stayed up all night reacting to every sound. He might have gotten an hour or two of sleep before morning, but really didn't care too much about that as he was just glad to see the sun shining again.

They got up and packed everything and went to breakfast. When they got back, Frank and Lucy started putting their things in the car and truck.

Ty got his and Caroline's luggage out of the room and turned in the keys. It was already hot and he was frustrated and tired of having to stand around waiting for them and their friends to finish their beer first thing that morning. It certainly did not help things out any.

It was a short ride to the airport. Ty got out of the car and unloaded his and Caroline's luggage.

The girls hugged and started to sadden a bit before they all said final good-byes and headed toward the boarding gate.

Ty didn't concern himself with who was boarding the plane. He sat down in his seat quietly and waited for the plane to take off.

He was in control this time, at least that's how he felt. Ty said a prayer and the jet began its long jog down the runway.

Caroline once again got all the positive attention from the staff on the flight home. The commercial jet was in the air and back down of the ground in no time at all.

Chapter 14

Jackie was at the airport awaiting Ty and Caroline's arrival. Jackie and Caroline were both very glad to see one another. Jackie's actions toward Ty were a bit standoffish, but peaceful. He understood how she felt since there had been very little communication between them over the previous two weeks.

The ride to the apartment was quiet. Ty didn't want to say anything wrong. There was so much on his mind and so much that had to be done. He had been baptized and was learning much about evil. He did not want to return to any bullshit.

Jackie didn't stay long at the apartment once Ty unpacked the car and brought all of their luggage inside. That hurt, but it was understandable. Jackie had to work the next day, after all. Plus, his Confidante was working on some things for him to do and Ty needed rest.

So he walked Jackie back out to her car after she and Caroline finished hugging and kissing, opened the car door for her and then held her tight and told her he loved her and would call her to make sure she made it home safely.

When she left, he went back to concerning himself with every possible scenario. He thought about everything, the things he had been told and the events that occurred before he left to go on the trip. And while he didn't want to be bothering with those things anymore, here he was, locked into a loop of worries on just those subjects.

He knew Jackie needed to move from that house as soon as possible, but if he kept at her to move, she would stay there just to be obstinate. It had to be her choice. All he could do was stay away and hope.

Back inside the apartment everything was still set up to protect Caroline and Ty from the evil that stalked them so relentlessly. Ty lit some candles, and then made sure Caroline was tucked away safely in bed. She had fallen asleep before he could even say good night to her.

It took Ty several attempts to reach Jackie at the old house by phone. She had stopped over at her mom's house before returning to the house on Newton St. Ty felt that Jackie's detour was just one of her ways of getting at him. She knew he would worry. Once they connected, Ty didn't say much other than he was glad to be home and loved her. He would talk to her tomorrow.

Before Ty went to sleep, he did get to talk to his Confidante and sure enough she had things that she wanted him to do the next day.

After he hung up the phone, Ty lay in bed and thought hard. The urgency was evident. Ty felt he was revealing, and had slowed the process of the young spirit's assault on his family's souls and minds. Nonetheless, he would return with a more aggressive attack, with lots of help.

Ty knew this for a fact and that made it more frightening, mind blowing, and more real with each encounter he and Joseph had with one another. Ty had no choice. Now Ty had identified the force, and now he knew that there were evil spirits, lost and unwanted souls, existing in the real world.

Ty was no longer fooled by the traps of drugs and sex in his life and since he was now taking a stand Joseph wanted him dead. Ty decided that all evil spirits are cowards. They get someone they can corrupt in life to do their dirty work and then destroy them.

Now he lay in bed, hoping that Jackie would soon see what he saw and would understand before it was too late. He prayed for her to run to the Higher Power, to hear, believe, live and confess, breathe the Word, and also for her to give her word, repent and be baptized. Then they would walk always with the Higher Power, no matter where they were.

He talked and prayed himself to sleep and when he woke up, Ty felt ready for the next challenge.

The next day Caroline didn't have any school as she was still out on break. She ate breakfast and then watched cartoons all morning. He waited until after lunch before letting her go out and play. Sometimes, neither of them could wait until it was time for her to go out and play. When that time came, out she went as Ty headed for the phone. It was time to find out what he had to do next.

His conversation with the Confidante was all about trapping young Joseph and putting him to rest before he finished off Ty.

She had some ideas on how they would try to get Joseph to come her way, and deal with him when he arrived. She already knew what she wanted to do and that was fine with Ty.

The Confidante had Ty put a pair of his underwear in a shoe box with a small piece of paper with his full name on it along with Jackie's and Caroline's. He also put a $100 bill in the box. He then closed it up and put it in a dark place, where he was to leave it overnight. This was one of the ways his Confidante said she would try to trap Joseph.

"What if I wake up in the morning and this box is full of evil? What am I supposed to do?" he asked.

"Whatever you do, don't open it," she warned.

Ty had already half prepared one box to send to her and now this second box.

Ty spoke out, "I don't like this idea at all. It's bad enough with the ring, and all the other things in my possession that I am not sure of, but now this."

"Relax and get those things together and put it all in the overnight mail and I will take a look at them," she suggested. "Stay positive and serious because we don't have much time."

"What are you going to do tonight?" he asked.

"Meditate on the box all night and pray it draws the energy that is needed to attract the evil spirit to it."

"Fine with me. Whatever it takes, I'll be sure to add my two cents tonight before I fall asleep with one eye open," Ty promised.

She just laughed and said, "You will have plenty of time to add to the cause. Your time is coming and the best thing for you to do is rest tonight because your faith has yet to be tested."

The end of their conversations always seemed like a mystery to Ty.

He locked up everything and called out to Caroline. She came running and met him at the car. They went to mail the box full of collected objects. Ty drove down the road and thought about the box in their apartment, and the box in his car. Now in truth, he could have cared less if he ever saw either one of those boxes again. Both boxes were like bombs to him. There had been no signs of unusual behavior in the past forty eight hours. The situation seemed to be like cancer in remission. He still couldn't help thinking about how he and his Confidante were trying to catch a young evil spirit in a box. It was time to put a spirit to rest.

He mailed the box to his Confidante via next day delivery, then left the post office but did not return to the apartment right away. He stayed away from the apartment for as long as possible. The box at the apartment would stay on his mind for the rest of the day and night.

He had his Confidante on the phone early the next day because he simply had to know whether the young spirit went for the money and scent in the box. His Confidante had awakened earlier and already knew the result of the attempt. Ty was hoping the experiment had worked, since the spirit had already tried using his ring to get at him.

The box didn't even draw a bite. Ty didn't know why, and was shook up. The box was just as worthless as any other empty box. Right when they felt they were onto something and advancing to the point of attack, they drew a blank. That really upset Ty, who stayed up all night, half expecting a grand entrance. A monster, perhaps. He had no idea what shape or form the evil young spirit was going to take when he arrived at Ty's apartment.

His Confidante told him he had to take that $100 bill back to the bank. It could not be spent; it would do much damage if it was spent.

Ty agreed and promised he would call back a little later in the morning. It was still too early for any news on the box of jewelry he sent her. Ty knew things would heat up as soon as she received his box. After he got back from the bank and deposited the $100 bill, he called her back.

The news was most definitely what he had expected. The ring was evil, contaminated in every way.

Ty told her to keep the ring, and whatever else was tainted. He didn't want those things around him.

The good things she sent back, telling him it was going to take all he had to draw this evil spirit to a place where it could be put to rest. "What exactly does she have in mind?" Ty wondered. She did not hesitate or even stutter when she told him it would require his total assets in a box along with the items that she spoke of earlier.

"My life savings!" Ty gasped.

She just quietly listened.

Ty sat the phone down and walked into the bedroom, picked up his King James Bible and read about Job.

Ty's entire life had been filled with lots of freedom after he had moved away from his childhood home to wander astray. His choice of association and his discipline had weakened. Ty was thinking about his slow self destruction and he hadn't forgotten the deceitfulness from others that helped bring on the growth of anger and lack of care into his life. Now it came down to the final test of his faith. He started getting a little restless, fumbling with the phone and the Bible. It was a good thing Caroline was outside playing as she did not need to see or hear him this way.

His Confidante continued listening and waiting quietly for Ty to get back on the phone as he read from the Bible and raved on.

Eventually, he got back on the phone and told her that he needed to read a few more verses. This time he read in Matthew, chapter 19, verses 21 and 22. "Jesus said unto him, 'If thou wilt be perfect, go and sell that thou hast, and give to the poor, and thou shalt have treasure in heaven: and come and follow me.' But when the young man heard that saying, he went away sorrowful: for he had great possessions." He then read on through verses 23 and 24 to try to get an explanation of his relations and relationship with verses 21 and 22. "Then said Jesus unto his disciples, 'Verily I say unto you, that a rich man shall hardly enter into the kingdom of heaven. And again I say unto you, it is easier for a camel to go through the eye of a needle, than for a rich man to enter into the kingdom of God.'" Instead of running away on the spot or hanging up the phone, he said simply, "Okay I'll do it."

"You are promised with this show of faith that great things will come," the Confidante said. The most important thing was that Ty's life was going to be spared and it would be his chance to stand by the Higher Power and put that young lost soul to rest.

Ty let her know it would take several days to get everything together. He had to make phone calls to the banks in and out of state that he was associated with and get what was in his possession and put it all into one cashier's check.

He made sure she knew that he understood everything and that he was okay with whatever had to be done. After receiving all of the information he needed, Ty hung up the phone and went on with his normal daily routine.

A week passed before he was ready to send his life savings and belongings to New Jersey.

He didn't tell anyone anything. He just followed everything to the last detail. This was something he could not share with anyone.

He was confident that by following the Confidante's plan that the young spirit would follow his scent—and the root of all evil— all the way to New Jersey where the Confidante and the church would await his arrival.

Ty phoned the Confidante the minute he mailed the package. The conversation was short.

"The package will fly next day air. I will talk to you in a few days," he said.

On his way back to the apartment after everything was done, Ty's mind started playing tricks on him. His faith was being challenged to the utmost, and he started questioning what had taken place.

He started thinking about all his great possessions that were gone. Once he got back to the apartment and sat down, he began reading the Bible and relating to Matthew's verse 22 again. "But when the young man heard that saying, he went away sorrowful: for he had great possessions."

He thought hard about how he could outsmart everyone. He came up with an idea and waited until the day after the Confidante received the box. Then he called the bank and canceled the cashier's check, reporting it lost.

A few days went by and he didn't hear from anyone, especially his Confidante, of course. He didn't want to call her because he knew what he had done.

Ty was not sure of what to do or what was going on, but he was nervous and wondering; something had to be happening. He thought of all kinds of things, but had to expect the worst. Somebody was going to get caught in some kind of scam, he thought. So he just waited.

The weekend came and he still didn't hear a thing. Now he was dying to see Jackie, and he was trying not to think about how bad a mistake he had made. He was really scared and felt stupid, but Jackie was what he wanted right then. He got in contact with her and she came over after work during the Fourth of July weekend. One thing led to another, and they were soon partying. It was just that easy for Ty to be overtaken. After all he had been through, how could this be happening to him? It was just like old times. There was so much pressure on Ty it was starting to warp him. He knew something was going to happen and it wasn't going to be good.

They were in the apartment and Ty thought he heard some kind of noise, a combination of breathing and pacing. Ty thought something was outside the front door, but did not say anything to Jackie. Instead he just played it off until he got a chance to look out the peephole.

Ty couldn't believe what he was seeing. It was a big black animal, a cat. He did a double-take, hoping it was just a cat, as the fish-eye lens in peepholes sometimes made things appear different than they were.

The cat started to walk away from the door very slowly, with it head down and its shoulder blades pointing straight up, practically protruding through its skin. The cat's tongue hung partially out of its mouth and its sides were bulging in and out, as if gasping for air. It was scarred by patches of frayed hair and Ty could tell that the cat was hurt badly.

Ty wanted Jackie to come and look, but did not want to mess up the good mood she was in. This large black cat continued walking away very slowly and then it stopped and looked back at Ty. He had seen that look before, a look he would never forget. He knew then the stunt he had pulled had caused a major problem, and all he could feel was danger. The cat spirit was Joseph; Ty realized Joseph had been badly wounded by the Confidante's people. As Ty watched the cat creature slink away, he knew that would be the last time he would ever see Joseph.

Ty walked away from the door and went into the room and checked on Caroline, and then returned to Jackie pretending that everything was all right.

The night and a day went by before Ty even had a clue as to the time. He still hadn't heard from his Confidante. What had happened to her? he wondered.

Ty went more or less into hiding. The weekend passed right along with church. Things just kept getting worse. He had lost faith and turned away from the Higher Power.

He was scared more than he ever had been. He felt nothing but the tightening tension. He couldn't take it anymore and called his Confidante. Sure enough, she had been waiting for his call.

She asked: "How long were you going to wait before you called me? Did anything strange happen?"

He confessed about the incident that took place on Friday night, along with what he saw and heard.

Then she spoke softly to him. Joseph had returned back home after almost killing her, along with several members of the congregation in New Jersey.

"Why did you do this to me and the church? You set me up and I was almost murdered!" she accused. "Why?"

Ty was scared speechless. He didn't know what to say or do. Everything that he had wondered about was answered.

She already knew what he had done, but she wanted Ty to confess in detail.

He did confess and the more he spoke of what he had done, the more it hurt her. She had so much trust and faith in Ty and he knew it remained, even after what he had done.

She said she had been fighting to get him another chance to show his faith even before he called.

The Confidante's priest wanted her to move on and leave him be.

The priest said Ty had no faith. He had come in to assist the Confidante with this problem and they had almost lost their lives. The priest told her that if Ty did not believe in the Higher Power and had no faith, then Ty must deal with this on his own. "We would only be risking our lives again," she reported the priest saying.

She told Ty that as of now he was in big trouble and Caroline's life was in great danger.

Ty began asking more detailed questions about this evil spirit who had attacked her and the others. She asked for what purpose he asked and cautioned him that it would be meaningless to discuss the subject.

Ty needed to know regardless. He had told her about this evil spirit and all the experiences he had been through. "Was it like I described, can it be so?"

"Yes, what you spoke of was true. The evil spirit smells," she answered.

She then described the scent the cat spirit produced in detail. The one thing he had never told her about was the spirit's scent. And her description of the stink was totally accurate. Ty became very still and quiet on the phone. He had made a big mistake.

"Are you still there?" she asked.

"Yes. Can you do your best to get me back into the church and convince the priest to give me another chance?" he whispered.

Again she told him that the priest was convinced that Ty's faith was as empty and worthless as the box they used to try and put that spirit to rest.

Ty then began pleading, swearing how sorry he was. He promised he wouldn't let her down again. Ty was so shook up that he really couldn't remember what he was saying to her as he said it.

Before she hung up the phone she told him that it was good that he had repented and confessed. She wanted Ty to pray and watch over Caroline every moment.

He promised her he wouldn't stop praying.

She said she knew he wouldn't. She also still believed in Ty for he had been chosen. But it wouldn't be so easy now for there was very little time left.

"Thanks and good-bye," Ty said, his voice choked with emotion.

When he hung up the phone, he had some decisions to make. Should he sit and have pity on himself or get on the phone and call the bank, and see how long it was going to take to make things right. He had to move fast because timing meant everything. The Confidante would get back to him in the next few days.

Those first couple of days were tough. Ty felt strange. He didn't sleep or eat well. His weight dropped and he felt generally poor. On the other hand, he was glad Caroline was okay.

His Confidante finally got back with him a couple of days later. He began asking question after question.

One of those questions was whether or not he was really in such extreme danger as he felt since last speaking to her.

"Yes! But, there isn't much left in this evil spirit right now because he was in a serious fight once he got here to New Jersey.

He will have to regroup. Believe it, there was much confusion," she said. "And there will be much more without him."

She warned Ty again that the young spirit was indeed after him and his family, and would stop at nothing to have them. She told him that as of now he was in the worst danger of his life and what he was feeling was real. "Joseph is not dead, he is weak but he has others to do his bidding and he will strike now, or soon, because your lack of faith allowed him to survive and you and your family are still in danger."

He was getting a second chance to make things right, but he only had two hours to do so. He had to get started right away.

She told him to call her and report his every move, and to speak to no one. "Hear this well: The church has let you back and the candles are lit once again for you. May the Higher Power be with you."

Ty hung up that phone and grabbed some things that he needed and left. He was going some distance away and it gave him time to think.

One thing Ty tried not to think about were the safety of Jackie and Caroline. He knew where they were. Jackie was at work and Caroline was in school. He just needed to handle his business and go with his instincts.

Will the young evil spirit chase me or take the chance and go right after Caroline, he wondered, vowing that he was not going to mess up this time.

The young spirit had come after Ty all the way and it had been intense. He couldn't believe it. Joseph shook him up to where he almost had a car accident on the Carmel Valley Road, which was pretty dangerous under the best of circumstances.

When Ty finally got to the Mid-Valley Center, he didn't mind the continuous pressure as long as he could make the deadline.

He did, but it didn't come easy. He used all the minutes he had.

Ty was relieved when he came out of the bank and made it to the Mail Boxes Etc. next door. The package was mailed. He even had the confirmation number.

Ty then made the call of his life to his Confidante. She answered the phone and they exchanged words. He gave her what she needed all over again, and just like that his life savings was gone again. What he sent was an attempt to save his family's lives.

Ty got himself something to eat and drink at the deli, and then drove back to the apartment. Now it was time to wait, hope and pray.

When he got there, he sat down but all he could think of were the last instructions he was given as to what to do and what not to do. Things were quiet around his place for a while.

A couple of days went by and Ty had only talked to Jackie once while she was at work. One thing she brought up in their conversation that made his day was the fact that she wanted to move right away from the old house.

Ty jumped on that conversation with both feet. "I will do whatever it takes to get you out of there," he vowed.

He asked her if the first of August 1997, which was two weeks away, would be too soon.

Jackie laughed and said, "Not soon enough!"

That brought a smile to Ty's face. "I'll talk to my landlord. I know of an apartment coming available within two weeks, on the other side of the complex that I'm staying in. I'll find out if anyone has put a deposit on it."

"Thank you," she said.

The very next day Ty visited the landlord. He took him over to look at the vacant apartment.

It was just right for Jackie, Jason and Ben. The landlord and Ty made a deal. He would hold the apartment for Jackie, and Ty put a deposit down to confirm it.

Ty couldn't wait to get on the phone to tell Jackie to start packing. He did just that and she was very happy, he could hear it in her voice.

Ty hung up the phone. He couldn't sit or stand still for a while, until the thought came over him once again regarding the status of his Confidante. He hadn't heard from her and decided to wait instead of calling.

One way or another he would know something soon. As long as his Confidante called within two weeks—before it became time to move Jackie's things out of that old house—he hoped all would be well.

He was not supposed to ever go over to the old house. Anyway, he had two weeks before that would take place so he was not going to think about it. He was sure his Confidante would get back with him and let him know what to do.

A couple more days went by and things were still quiet around both the house and his apartment.

Jackie never said anything about the old house and Ty didn't care to ask. He didn't want to start anything. Then he finally got the call he'd been waiting for. He could barely hold on to the phone because of his nerves.

The soft-spoken Confidante wouldn't go into details, but said things had been done and it was the time to move on.

He tried to get her to talk about it, but she had other things she wanted to discuss with Ty.

She told him it was time to do away with his past, all thirty-nine years. What she told him to do was to make sure he had a candle lit every day for two hours for one year. She told him to get thirty-nine small single candles, these he would not burn, but take those and wrap each one with a dollar bill and put them in a shoe box in a dark place for one year and never go near it or open it. That was easy for him to do, but there were other things he had to worry about and one was staying clean.

Ty asked his Confidante about Jackie and she told him that he must think about himself, and be strong for Jackie.

"Jackie will have to choose her own direction and when she's ready she will make the right decisions. And if she doesn't, you are not to follow. You must go in the right direction or things will most definitely go for the worse," she predicted.

Chapter 15

Ty told his Confidante about the move he and Jackie were planning, and asked her if he could help Jackie move out of the old house. He gave his Confidante the date and the details and she told him to go there and help, but to be out by dark.

They both laughed. "You won't have to worry about that because this will go down as the fastest move ever, and whatever is there after dark will stay there," Ty promised.

The Confidante explained that things had been difficult and she was tired and hadn't had much sleep. It was time for her to get the rest she needed. Ty understood and told her he loved her deeply and would be in contact later. He assured her that he would get right on the things that she told him to do. Ty thanked her profusely and the conversation ended.

He and Caroline then left the apartment to obtain the one dollar bills. Ty was somewhat relieved, but in the back of his mind, he still had the one thing he knew was going to be hard to deal with—getting high.

When they returned to the apartment, Caroline watched TV while Ty wrapped each candle with a dollar bill and put a rubber band around them tightly. Each candle represented a year of his life.

Ty thought of those past years and tried to remember as much as he could, the bad with the good. The bad memories, he did not care to think of as much, but the good ones brought smiles to his face. Ty was hoping this was it and that he would learn something from all this. He put those candles in their box in a dark corner of the storage area and closed the door. By nightfall he was ready for a good night's rest, and he and Caroline turned in early for bed after dinner.

Ty didn't remember falling asleep that night, but when the sun shone through and showed signs of morning, he got up quickly to light a candle.

At breakfast Caroline asked, "Is the evil spirit going to come to our apartment again?" That caught Ty off guard because he had been watching everything he said around her.

Ty told her not to be concerned and to enjoy the rest of her summer break. He didn't want her worrying about that kind of thing. She then asked about Jackie living in the old house. Ty told her that Jackie was moving soon and was going to be living near them. That made her very happy and she could not wait for the move.

"No more weird old house," she said.

Ty smiled and they both laughed.

The next couple of weeks passed quickly and as moving day grew near, Ty often touched bases with his Confidante for reassurance.

The day of the move he made sure they were armed with crosses and their special rocks. Ty didn't take his car, he used a small truck that he had borrowed, and he had plenty of assistance. Jason, Ben, John, Carla, Caroline and Jackie all helped out.

Ty didn't have to explain to the kids why he had to be out of the old house by dark. They had all heard the stories and did not like the place either. Ty walked into the old house first and felt slightly unbalanced. He could see now what had inspired the sudden change in Jackie's wanting to move. There was a sense of great confusion within the walls. Joseph was gone, defeated by the Confidante, but something was still a mess.

He thought after all the frights he had had with this house while he stayed in it, whatever residual evil was left would be frightened of him. He didn't stand still long enough to find out, however.

Ty moved things out of that house so fast his helpers had to run to keep up. He was racing against time and whatever else might occur.

He made a few trips from the house to the apartment and as darkness grew near he had to end the move and leave things behind in the shed outside. Maybe, one day, he would try to come back for them.

When he finally brought the last box into the apartment, Ty began blessing every corner of the place with holy water and prayers.

It was so nice to know the move was over, but he still felt that as long as he was with Jackie his problems were not over.

That night he sat around with the kids and Jackie, enjoying the new apartment until it became time for Ty and Caroline to go back to their apartment.

The next day when they got up, the first thing Caroline wanted to do was to go visit Jackie's new apartment.

Ty let her go after breakfast and he stayed behind to take care of the chores.

After he finished, he called Jackie to make sure she was up before he came over to say hi and see how the first night at the new apartment went.

Ty came into the apartment looking around as if it was too good to be true. He wasn't convinced that their troubles were gone, especially with that weird sofa of Jackie's around. He never did like that sofa, there was something about it and he just could not figure out what it was. He got a bad feeling from it, but he didn't say anything. He wanted to leave things alone and let Jackie enjoy something positive for a change.

Jackie had to work a little later that afternoon at the restaurant so she lay around as long as she could. She slept well and was very happy with the new living arrangement. Once she left for work, Ty tried putting things in place around the apartment. He knew when Jackie got off from work she was going to party a little bit, a sort of celebration or house warming. And he knew he would be joining her.

The re-united lovers stayed up almost all night and another Sunday went by without Ty making any contact with church. The church was weighing heavily on his mind since he hadn't been back.

Each time Ty missed church the guilt grew within him. It got to the point where he avoided everyone when leaving the apartment, as he did not wish to run into anyone he knew. Not the way he was looking. Anyone who knew him would be able to tell he was not taking care of himself. Ty heard that the minister's wife had been asking around for him and that only made it worse.

Ty had to give it another try and get himself together. School was starting back for the kids and he needed to make some changes. Caroline always started out slowly in the beginning of a school year, and Ty needed to be there for her. He could not be staying up half the night partying and then keep it all together.

He also had to deal with Jackie's boys again now that she lived in the same apartment complex, and that was difficult.

Ty finally decided to call his older sister Pat and see if he and Caroline could start going to her church. He also obtained a membership at the gym where his brother Kenneth worked.

Ty and Caroline started going to church again and things started looking up for them. On Ty's second time in Pat's church he got called on to help out with the Higher Power's supper and with the collections. He was so nervous the first time that it was noticeable. Pat told him after he had helped out with the Higher Power's supper and collections a second time that she was proud of him and that he looked like he had won back his faith.

The minister came up to Ty after church and told him that he was very thankful, and the church felt blessed that Ty was attending the services. It felt good to have a man of spiritual beliefs recognize his spirit. Ty thanked the minister.

As he walked alongside Pat he asked, "How did I look today?"

She told him that he shined brightly in church and encouraged him to keep it up. Ty was not sure how long he could keep anything up anymore. In fact, he was just living day to day.

A month went by before Ty slipped into darkness once again. He quit working out at the spa and stopped going to church and he was now wasting more of his rent and food money. He couldn't even drive his car because he didn't have the money to register it. He and Caroline were just barely getting by.

By then it was late in the year, November 1997. Ty had spoken with his Confidante a couple of times but didn't tell her everything or much of anything for that matter. He'd sometimes stay out late into the early morning looking for some dope to bring back to the apartment. Most of the time he took Caroline along with him if she wasn't asleep already because Jackie would want to go too and he didn't like leaving Caroline alone at the apartment watching TV.

Ty did crazy things to get high, but nothing compared to what he had seen and heard others do, at least not yet. Things were getting worse for him and his future suddenly looked bleak.

Ty kept telling himself that he was going to get away before it became too late. He continued going places where he had no business being, risking everything. Ty had been flirting with prison or death for a while now. They seemed like the only destinations he could picture and picture them he really could. It became hard to stay straight, but Ty managed to keep a candle burning each day trying to keep his past in the past.

It was now obvious that he and Jackie were bad for each other and living as close together as they did made things worse. They were pulling against one another. When one of them tried to do right, the other would screw up so they eventually made the wrong chose. There really wasn't a chance to go straight for any long periods at a time.

By the time the month of November passed, the only thing Ty vaguely remembered from that month was that he had had Thanksgiving dinner with his whole family.

By December, Ty was back in touch with those uneasy feelings. He knew right away the feelings were as bad as before, and the anticipation of some awful event brought him much suspense every time he heard a noise.

On a very cold night in December, he and Jackie were partying and ran out of drugs, so Ty left the apartment on his bike, leaving Jackie to watch over Caroline while she slept. Ty ended up staying gone longer than Jackie or he expected. Once he was out looking for drugs, he wouldn't come back until he had found some.

When Ty finally got back to his apartment, he got the feeling that something out of the ordinary was happening. One thing he didn't want was to have to deal with were those spirits again.

Ty carried his bike up the steps and froze once he reached the top. There were noises coming from inside his apartment, the same sounds he'd heard at the old house.

He leaned his bike up against the railing and went for the door quickly, but had no key. So he knocked but there was no answer. He went to each window and could see both Caroline and Jackie in the bed. The windows were slightly opened but the safety locks were intact.

Ty called out to Jackie but the awful sounds coming from inside the apartment drowned out his desperate calls for her to awaken. He couldn't rouse either one and presumed that something had happened while he was gone. He went into a panic and began running from one side of the building to the other thinking that someone besides Jackie and Caroline were still in his apartment. He leaned his bike up against the door and tried to be as quiet as possible. He was afraid that if he woke up the neighbors and they didn't recognize him, the police would show up. And he did not want that.

Ty could not let anyone leave that apartment without catching them. When he ran to the other side of the building, he knew that if someone opened the front door the bike would fall over and let him know that someone was coming out.

He tried again and again to wake Jackie, but the noises coming from within his apartment grew into a massive roar louder and he noticed that Jackie started to move around a bit in the bed, and sounds began emanating from her. He became alarmed to the point of wanting to break down the door. He knew he just had to get in.

Ty finally managed to remove the window completely and climbed in through it. Once inside, he checked everything out. Nobody was there except Jackie and Caroline, both in a deep sleep. But Ty couldn't relax. He continued to pace back and forth in that little apartment until he was able to pinpoint the location where the noise was coming from—the closet and on the other side of the wall was where he kept those candles with the dollar bills wrapped around them in the storage. Ty did not go near the box. He just hoped that it would remain tightly secured.

After Ty settled down a bit, he put the window back in place. Then, instead of waking Jackie, he sat down and did some thinking. What was happening here? Revenge was a thing to be expected. Ty needed to confirm his thoughts. He knew the evil spirits from that old house would seek revenge on Jackie for her betrayal of young Joseph. He was not going to stand for any more threats on Caroline's soul or his own. It would not be left unsettled.

That morning when Jackie woke up she began telling Ty about this bad dream that she had. She was also having bad feelings about Ben. With it being early and Caroline still asleep, he asked her to join him on the couch in the living room. He asked her to relate the whole dream. He could tell she had really been touched by this dream, and this feeling she had was genuine.

She started to cry. Ty told her to calm down, that it was only a dream. She insisted that it wasn't just a dream. As she became more upset, Jackie explained that the dream reflected feelings she had been having during her days at work and while driving in the car. She felt something would happen to Ben, and she felt that it was going to be fatal. That most definitely got Ty's attention.

He explained to her that she shouldn't worry so hard and he would go check on Ben a little later that morning. It was time Ty got some rest. He lay back on the sofa and Jackie went into the kitchen to fix some coffee. Ty wondered if she even remembered the events of the last few hours; he wasn't even at the apartment and hadn't had any sleep.

When Ty woke up, Caroline and Jackie were watching TV. He looked at the time, noting that only three hours had passed. He still got up and went into the bathroom to wash up, knowing that he must get over to Jackie's apartment before Ben left that morning.

He opened the front door to leave and was startled by his bike falling into the apartment. Jackie started to ask why the bike was there, but Ty cut her off and laughed. "You really don't want to know how or why my bike was there," he assured her. Ty moved the bike and closed the door behind him. He went to her apartment to have a talk with Ben.

Ty walked into the apartment to catch Ben just in time, as he was dressed and ready to leave for the day.

"Good morning, Ben."

"Good morning to you Ty. Is there something wrong?" Ben asked.

"Well since you mentioned it, there is something I would like to talk to you about. Your mom is worried about you. She says she been having bad feeling and these dreams she's having about you aren't any good. I want you to take heed and just be careful, okay," Ty pleaded.

"I will, especially with all that has been going on, I can see she still is a little unsettled. Thanks, Ty," Ben mentioned as he was walking out the door.

Ty and Jackie meanwhile continued getting high back and forth in one another's apartments, and the feelings of danger kept growing more real as each weekend passed.

It was long past time to call his Confidante, and Ty knew it. He knew what she was going to tell him, but he had to hear it anyway.

Ty contacted her and talked for several minutes. Then she spoke: "I know what you have gotten yourself back into. You chose that way. If you continue, it is no one's fault but your own. Now it is on Jackie to make the correct decisions." The Confidante had once told Ty that when Jackie was ready to talk or when she recognized what was happening to her own life then she would give the Confidante a call. But that was going to be between her and Jackie. "Your final destination is still up to you. Choose it wisely."

Ty's Confidante was disappointed in him and he could tell. She was cold and straightforward. He had expected it to be that way. It was quiet for a while on the phone. She reminded Ty of how important Christmas was going to be for Caroline. "Don't blow it," she warned him.

Ty got off the phone and decided to start putting the Christmas lights up. He still had time before he had to pick Caroline up from school and wanted to surprise her on the last day before Christmas break.

Just as he finished hanging up all the lights, he heard the phone ring. It was the phone company calling to inform him that his service was going to be cut off because there was an outstanding unpaid phone bill from the old house, which was in Ty's name. There was nothing he could do. When Ty hung up the phone, he just sat and said to himself, "What a nice Christmas present from Jason." Jason, it seems, had been calling a girlfriend long distance and ran up the phone bill. Jackie had tried very hard to keep him off the phone, but he somehow managed to keep making the calls. Unfortunately, Ty did not have $500 for the phone company.

His calls to and from his Confidante were over. He had no phone and there was no way he could call her from Jackie's apartment. Ty made it through Christmas and Caroline received a few nice gifts and was happy and content.

But in spite of everything the partying between Tyrone and Jackie continued. Ty decided that he would make a New Year's resolution not just for himself, but for Jackie as well. She told him in no uncertain terms that she would stop partying when she was good and ready. Ty became very angry at this point and threatened to pack up one day and leave town.

Ty got so wasted on New Year's Eve that a few days passed him right on by. Everything was going to go, they were going to lose everything, he thought and complained, and became more frustrated than ever. He didn't care, but he kept those candles burning each day.

So much money had been wasted that Ty and Caroline were spending a lot more time at Jackie's apartment trying to save on the bills, food, electricity and water. But it didn't help; they just bought more drugs. Things were degenerating. Nobody worked except Jackie.

The boys always had a lot of company at the apartment. Even Jason's girlfriend made it down from the city and now stayed at Jackie's apartment full-time. Ty couldn't do or say anything about it because his own apartment didn't have any food in it and he couldn't afford to get kicked out of Jackie's place again. Ty and Jackie only went to his apartment to get high.

Ty really couldn't stand it in either apartment. The noise at his apartment where he kept those candles with the dollars wrapped around them was crazy, the apartment was unbearable to get high in and try to stay calm, no way, it was too frightening. When he was alone at Jackie's apartment, he could feel the evil in it. He always kept an eye on that sofa bed in her living room, feeling there had to be something wrong with that piece of furniture.

Jason, Ben and their friends were coming and going from her apartment, smoking and drinking. The neighbors were watching and starting to talk.

One day Ty came out and caught management watching Jackie's apartment. It was just a matter of time before something bad went down. Ty told Jackie about it and she talked to Jason and Ben, but Jason could not have cared less. As long as Ty and Jackie were getting high, he refused to stop. He would do whatever he wanted to do. Both apartments were being watched very closely by now.

Ty and Jackie were now driving her car with no registration and had been stopped by the police twice in the month of January. Jackie told the police she had already paid by mail and had not yet received the registration papers back each time they were stopped. Ty would just sit with his palms sweating and hope for the best.

The police were not concerned about her registration. They were checking for warrants and looking for a reason to search the car for drugs. Ty and Jackie were regulars out in the streets in the wee hours of the morning and it was obvious what they were doing. But nothing changed, except they decided not to drive her car after dark anymore. Ty started riding his bike and even then he got stopped and had several close encounters with the police.

It continued to look like the walls were closing in on him. There was so much time passing, days and weeks of just getting high and Ty was deep into making the wrong choices. He hadn't talked to his Confidante since December and really did not want her to know what he had been doing. Besides, if she wanted to read into what he was up to, he was sure she could do so as long as his candles were burning each day, and they were.

Ty had a 40th birthday coming up soon and he wanted to get back on track. He gave Jackie the old "Life Begins at 40" speeches. Ty wanted to have one last party.

April 17, 1998 came and went. It had been a party all right and more parties followed. By the end of April, Ty got his car registered. Now, with the registration taken care of, there was no real reason for the police to stop them in Ty's car. It was back to business as usual.

Ty really didn't care. The police were going to have to bust him red-handed now. He knew for sure the landlord and the police were working together, so he gave his 30-day notice to vacate his apartment. Ty said he would leave the state one day and this would just be one more step toward doing that. Ty had also been on probation for a while; he'd been arrested way back before they all moved into that old house and he knew the police did not need a search warrant to enter his apartment. It was just a matter of time before they were going to exercise that authority.

Ty's apartment had now turned into a cold unwanted place anyway. Every time he went there for clothes or to try to get high, he would hear more weird noises in the walls. The noises were unbelievable, especially those coming from the storage room. He just couldn't get comfortable there at all.

He figured he might as well move into Jackie's apartment until he made his final move out of state. He knew the police couldn't walk right into Jackie's apartment. There would be some kind of warning. Better still, it was an upstairs apartment with no easy access to the front door. Ty felt a little safer there—from the police, at least.

He had been trying to put some pressure on Jackie to move with him. He knew she had to leave town or lose everything including her freedom and her life. But he knew he had to be cool about the moving topic. She had to make up her own mind. Either way, Ty had to leave town.

He moved his things out of the apartment during the night into Jackie's storage and stashed some things in her apartment. He tried to be as slick as possible.

Two weeks went by and he and Jackie were at their worst. Her dreams were recurring and they were more realistic than ever. Ty thought something was happening, but couldn't figure what that was.

The second week in May, Jackie's nightmare became a reality. One Thursday night, he and Jackie were upstairs in her apartment letting it all hang out when Ty thought he sensed something burning.

He leaned over the banister and looked downstairs where Ben and Caroline were sleeping. Ben looked to be fighting in a deep sleep on the sofa, so Ty called Jackie to look. They watched him for a short while until they both hurried downstairs to the sofa. He could hear the fire in the sofa, which he had placed up against the door. He thought someone had set the sofa on fire by sliding something underneath the front door. Ty quickly checked under the sofa and all around it. Jackie just stood there in shock not uttering a word.

Ty tried to wake Ben. He felt the boy's body and it was burning hot. Ty became nervous and excited and called out to Ben, waking him. Ty asked him if he was hot and Ben moaned as if he were in pain.

"I'm so hot," he moaned. Ty snatched the boy off the sofa and placed him on the floor, watching him closely.

Ben felt normal a short time later, and fell back asleep.

All of a sudden the sounds of fire stopped. Ty now knew exactly what was happening. Revenge. He remembered what his Confidante had told him about all the spirits inhabiting the old house that had once lived there with young Joseph.

The spirits were after Jackie because she had switched sides and was now working with Ty. He took something from the spirits and they were going to take back. He began explaining it all to Jackie. She became very frightened, but she believed him.

Ty went back upstairs but Jackie remained downstairs for a while, watching over the kids. Once Ty got upstairs, he heard a noise outside the window. He looked outside there on the ledge, and was instantly reminded of a night at the old house on Newton Street. That horrible night came back to him. He had been alone there to prepare for war and fought for his life all night long in that burning supernatural fire, when an ancient evil figure stared at him. It had looked like a wicked witch with a feline head. He saw the image of that wicked figure with its hair standing up, like as if it had been struck by lighting. And the weird noises it made! He saw this at the old house, and now here it was again outside Jackie's apartment window. Surrounding this evil looking visage were images of large, disfigured, mummy-like shapes. The living dead, he presumed.

Despite his paralyzing fear, Ty fought to disguise it. The apartment was surrounded and Ty could sense that the spirits were planning to attack. He now became both afraid and angry, and began yelling at the entities. Hearing him, Jackie called out: "Who are you talking to?"

"Just talking to myself," he responded.

Ty was warning the entity that it better not mess with him or Caroline. If it did, Ty promised he would do whatever it took to get rid of them as he had with Joseph. "This is between you and Jackie," he mumbled, and continued staring directly in the eyes of the evil cat witch looking spirit until Jackie came upstairs.

Ty quit getting high for the night. He knew he couldn't go to sleep. It had been just too close a call for him to sleep oblivious to what was going to happen the rest of the night.

He sat down and thought about whether or not he should say anything to Jackie, and decided not to. He simply waited to see how she handled the rest of the night.

There was danger in the air and he knew it. Ty sat very still watching and listening. He knew she would soon be seeing and feeling everything that he felt.

Jackie sat down but not for long. She soon got up and started looking out the window. This was her problem, Ty said to himself.

Neither of them got any sleep, and she had to work the next morning.

Jackie made it to work after lunch the next day. Ty took Caroline to school and then went over to his apartment and started cleaning until it was time to go back and pick her up from school.

Ty had gotten so high again that he became paranoid. It got bad at Jackie's apartment as the sun started to set. He dialed 911 but hung up before the operator could answer.

The 911 operators called back and he begged them not to send a patrol car over to Jackie's apartment. He told the operator that Caroline had been playing with the phone. The police came anyway, and Ty was so high he did not know what to do.

Ty ran to Kenneth's apartment and knocked on his door. Kenneth and his wife Kelly both answered the door. Ty began talking rapidly and pushed himself into their apartment. Kenneth didn't know what was going on. All he heard as Ty headed for his bathroom was Ty pleading for Kenneth to tell the police that he had been at Kenneth's apartment all day. Then Ty jumped into his shower. Kenneth stood in shock as Ty started taking a shower, and then came out of the bathroom naked. Kenneth rushed to him with a towel.

"Hey man, you can't walk around in my house like that. Kelly will be back anytime now," Kenneth protested.

Kelly had gone to see what was going on over at Jackie's apartment and didn't see any police, so she came right back. Both Kenneth and Kelly were angry. Ty was told to get the hell out and not ever come back. Kelly threatened to call the police, but instead she called Jackie. Jackie and Caroline had to come get Ty. He didn't want it to be that way. He did not want to believe it, that he had been told not to ever come back. Before he left, he shook Kenneth's hand and hugged Kelly. She hugged Ty like he was dirt. Ty looked straight into their eyes and told them both that he would never set foot in their apartment again.

Jackie and Caroline showed up and Ty left with them both headed back to Jackie's apartment. Ty told Jackie what he had done, how he ran into Kenneth's apartment looking crazy. They both laughed and she told him that he was crazy.

The police had come immediately after he left, Jackie explained, and they followed him around the corner.

Ty sat down and thought about it. The police were after him. It was time to leave town. It had to end one way or the other! He hadn't come down off of his high yet, either.

Ty tried to salvage some pity from Jackie. He began talking about his family and how even they wanted him to leave town. This was untrue, but he could understand how it might be the case, given their tragic family history.

Jackie told him that he had a lot more to be concerned about than Kenneth and Kelly. It wasn't the first time they had made him feel badly. She told him that he needed to stop walking around the apartment complex late at night loaded and looking suspicious or else he was going to wind up in jail.

Ty finally came down off his high and made it through the night, but the thought of those evil spirits and the police kept him on the edge.

The situation then became even worse. It seemed as if there was no stopping him and Jackie from getting high. The next day he walked out of her apartment and noticed the police were on the grounds of the complex. He walked to his apartment and just as he opened the door the landlord showed up and informed him that he could not "loiter on the property" once he moved out of his apartment. Ty didn't expect that and simply nodded numbly. He had emptied and cleaned out his apartment already, so he hurried and locked up his door. Ty did not give the landlord a chance to look inside his apartment as he knew the landlord would take away his keys immediately. Ty had a few more days left in the month and was not about to surrender a minute of his remaining time.

Chapter 16

Ty hustled back over to Jackie's apartment, feeling desperate, lost and empty, his life like a runaway train.

He kept peeking out the windows and wondering if anyone was going to come check Jackie's apartment looking for him. Ty was not only hiding from the police but from the landlord as well. I can't stay here, he told himself. So he closed himself up in her apartment and every little noise drove him to a state of panic. He needed to get out of her apartment.

Ty decided to go to a house where a guy by the name of Aaron stayed. This guy wasn't straight in any sense of the word. As a matter of fact, he was worse off than Ty. He was just another of the lowlifes Ty bought drugs from.

When Ty got to Aaron's house, the dealer came out and got into Ty's car.

"What do you need?" he asked.

"I was just hanging out," Ty said.

Ty drove Aaron around since he had a few places he needed to go. It wound up taking all afternoon, but Ty didn't have to pick Caroline up from school as she had slept in with everyone else that morning and was at the apartment with Ben.

There really was a purpose behind his visit with Aaron. Aaron had angered Ty many times over. He would either try to proposition Ty every chance he got with his preference of sex acts for a little extra dope, or just flat out make fun of Ty in front of Jackie. Ty waited until it started getting a little late toward sundown before he spoke his piece.

"There is something I want to show you," he said.

"Yeah? What's that?" Aaron asked.

"First break out the stuff; I know you have it."

Aaron smiled. "I have it, but I ain't going to let you have any because you might kill us both with your driving," he responded.

Ty just laughed, "I won't do anything stupid while I'm driving."

"Let's make a deal," Aaron suggested.

"I am not gonna make any deals with you. I know what you're up to and all about. I've known from the first time I laid eyes on you. No chance here, Aaron."

"The Hell with you," he said.

"I am here to try and shed some light into this dark and nasty life of yours that you seem to think is so cool. I have something to prove to you and to myself. What you are about to witness, you will never forget," Ty promised.

"Whatever. Prove it then," Aaron shrugged as he was breaking out his pipe and putting a rock in it.

Ty drove him up to the cemetery—where nothing was happening and the dead had the decency to stay in their graves and mausoleums, at least for the moment—and started smoking crack. After a few hits off the pipe from both of them the car filled with sickly-sweet smoke. Ty then prepared for all kinds of weird things to start happening.

Ty told Aaron that there were going to be lights flashing and sirens, as if the police were coming, and they would be having some uninvited guests riding along with them. Ty started laughing as if cheering it on while he pulled over. The rear car doors opened and closed, followed by a very foul smell. Ty teased and asked Aaron if he had crapped in his pants or what. The air in the car had gotten very cold, dry and foul.

The atmosphere became thin and tense and Ty's chest contained what felt like his last breath.

Ty looked over at Aaron, "How do you like me now?" he asked with a strange smile. He just wanted to make sure Aaron was living it with him. He could see that Aaron was getting the full effect. He began panting and moving around the car, terrified and begging Ty to cut it out.

"I'm not doing anything. The living dead and all the evil spirits on the face of this earth are just partying with us."

Aaron didn't respond. "I want to go," was all he said.

But Ty wouldn't leave just yet. He waited until he was sure that Aaron had had enough.

"This is something I experienced in the past and I had to fight hard myself before being overwhelmed by what was happening,"

Ty told him. At this point Ty wasn't much afraid of the spirits, any more, knowing the real danger was his lifestyle and the cops.

"Please, man, just stop this shit and take me home," Aaron pleaded.

Ty did attempt to discourage the special effects, but everything intensified as he drove Aaron home. His passenger sat quietly as the spectral assault continued throughout the ride back to Aaron's place. Before the car came to a complete stop, Aaron had already opened the door and spilled out onto the sidewalk. He left his bag of drugs behind, and Ty could tell that Aaron would experience at least a temporary reformation.

As Aaron stumbled up the driveway, Ty began preaching at him. "You must do all you can to change your life or else." Aaron's head merely nodded up and down in passive agreement.

It happened just as Ty predicted.

Ty drove off as Aaron reached his front door and headed home. He was still determined to get away; to get out of this town! He had just scared several doses of Hell out of both Aaron and himself. Ty had taken Aaron for a spin and a small legion of the living dead came along for the ride.

That night after he made it back to Jackie's, she asked, "Where have you been?" Ty showed her the bag full of drugs and it didn't matter where he'd been. She was on the pipe in less than a minute but before Ty took his first hit, he told her what the landlord had said about him being banned from the complex once he moved out.

She shrugged, declining to respond and instead reported the news that Jason and his girlfriend were moving back up to the city in a couple of days.

"Good. That means less traffic in and out of this apartment."

Jackie then dropped a bombshell, reporting that she was ready to move.

"This is a surprise. When?" Ty asked numbly.

"I'll give my 30-day notice on the first of July," she said.

Ty began to feel a twitching anxiety in his jaw.

"In the meantime, *I* have to figure out where I'm going to stay. I don't see how the landlord can stop Caroline from staying at her mom's apartment, but I am going to have to lay low."

The rest of the night he and Jackie smoked and talked, while he constantly looked out the windows. Time was the one thing that kept right on passing.

Jason did leave and school was soon out for the summer. Holding down two jobs, back to back, however was starting to wear Jackie down. As time passed she was going in late on one gig and calling in sick on the other with regularity. Ty's month had run out, but he didn't leave Jackie's. He just stayed out of sight the best he could around the complex.

Toward the end of June 1998, Ty went into the office and gave the landlords Jackie's notice of intent to vacate the apartment in 30-days. He caught the landlords off guard, showing up in the office like that. He was trying to stay one step ahead. They wanted to know in detail what Ty and Jackie were doing and where they were moving. They were nosy and surprised.

Ty played it off and told them what they wanted to hear. Knowing he had satisfied them made things a little easier and from then on he did not have to hide. He was working on their move and the landlords got used to the sight of Ty coming and going.

The word was out all over town that Tyrone and Jackie would be leaving soon. Everyone had something to say on the subject. Ty isn't going anywhere, some said. Ty was washed up and nothing but a big talker, others insisted. Their leaving meant a loss of income to some people because Ty was buying so much dope from them, and to others it meant the fear of their own darkness coming to light. The longer Ty stayed, the longer he would divert police attention away from them. With Ty gone, the spotlight would fall on someone else. The percentage of people, whether they were business owners, or parents, were either selling it or using it, and as long as Ty's name was out there as a one-time heavy player on the way down, it made it all the better for them. They could point the finger and keep Ty's name circulating throughout the town and away from themselves.

There were still others who would try to be sincere and asked to go with Ty and his family, sort of like on the buddy plan. But the last thing Ty needed was passengers who didn't have enough sense to leave on their own.

There was one lady in particular. She and Jackie grew up together on the same street. Donna stood out in Ty's mind as she constantly pleaded to come along. It was a shame, but Ty had made up his mind; she had to make it out of there on her own and she had nothing left but a crack pipe. A one time beauty, she had taken a wrong turn for a single woman with a son, got mixed up in the drug infested and forsaken town it had become.

There were many so called friends, and when they called to see if Ty wanted to buy some drugs for the road he would preach so much to them that they never called back. When unexpected guests dropped by to see if there was any packing going on—or just to be corruptive—Ty would burn incense. That got the spirits' attention and brought the dead to the apartment. The human guests wouldn't stick around long after that.

Jackie was always at work, which gave Ty plenty of time to sit and think about the town. In a way he had fun playing games, being cold with anyone who passed his way and telling it like it was. At the same time, it challenged the tolerance of his nerves. Most definitely the challenge was on! Jackie and Ty still had 30 days to go.

Some time ago Ty had been placed on probation, after getting into trouble with the law. He was pulled over for a cracked taillight. Unfortunately, among his possessions at the time was a rusty, non-functioning hand gun, probably the oldest, least threatening weapon the officer had ever seen. Ty was in the process of transporting it back to his house. But they were in Jackie's car, cracked taillight and all, and the gun was with him.

Ty was sentenced to 18-months in prison, five years probation and a $6,000.00 fine. He also had to report to DUI-related classes for three month and three more months of drug school. On top of it all he could not possess any type of weapon for ten years. The only silver lining for Ty was the fact that his drug dealer had run out of drugs moments before Ty reached his house. Ty was pulled over right after leaving the dealer's house.

Jackie pointed out that it had been a good thing Ty hadn't been drinking that night. He would never forget her saying that after his sentencing. But he seriously felt it had been a good thing one of his so-called gang-banger friends hadn't been the one to pull him over that night and put a cap in him. The 18-month sentence was suspended and he ended up doing 45 days. The rest of his sentence stood, and the probation was still very real.

Ty had a brother-in-law on the police force. It was obvious this man knew what was going on and what Ty's life consisted of at the time, but there was nothing he could do about it. When Ty faced Officer Martin on the streets, the policeman followed him stop sign to stop sign. When Martin was on duty, he would always pull up next to Ty and ask him if he was all right. Of course Ty would say he was. Officer Martin would tell him to take care, and would always remind him that his niece loved him and that would be it; he would drive away. It gave Ty both a sense of strength and the chills. Now he sat in Jackie's apartment reminiscing about those times and applying the situation to the present. If he went down now, it would be a sacrifice. It would be the talk of the town forever. The time had gotten away from him and he had been feeling those sentiments for some time as Jackie walked in the door early from work that night with dinner from the restaurant.

Ty came downstairs and Jackie seemed to be a little excited to see him. The food drew Ben and Caroline's attention until Jackie started talking about taking a trip to Las Vegas.

Ty and Jackie knew that an old high school friend of Jackie's lived in Las Vegas. Jackie announced that she was making arrangements for them to visit Vegas for a few days. It now seemed real to Ty that a move was going to take place—but Las Vegas? Well, if that's where she wanted to live then let's do it, Ty decided.

The trip was made that weekend. Jackie, Ben, Caroline and Ty went to Las Vegas and stayed four days. It was a good trip. Jackie even broke down and selected a location where she wanted to live there. It was determined that they would be back to Las Vegas in 30-days, bags and all. They informed their friends who lived in Vegas that they were serious. Ty really, truly hated the idea of returning to California.

As soon as they returned to Jackie's apartment on the 3rd of July, Ty started calculating how much money they would need once it was time to move to Las Vegas.

Ty didn't have any savings, of course. Everything was gone between the crack and the cashier's check. All he could count on was his monthly check that was deposited directly to his account. And Jackie was still working two jobs.

He got all the figures together on paper and showed it to Jackie, who was in bed. Ty figured around $5,000.00 would do it.

Then there was this question of whether they would get out of town without blowing every cent of it on the pipe. They would find that out sooner than later.

Ty tossed and turned half the night knowing they would not leave with that kind of money. He decided to order a truck and paid for it in advance. His check was already in the bank, but he would have to wait until after the 4th when everything opened back up to get at it. At least he would get the truck out of the way and then all he would need was gas money to get them out of town. He went on tossing and turning himself to sleep.

The next day, July 4, was the start of a party. That night Ty and Jackie were hitting the pipe hard when all of a sudden she panicked. Jackie wanted to leave the apartment and go for a walk immediately. She became terrified and would not even wait for Ty to put on his shoes and walked quickly out the door.

Ty told the kids to stay inside and took off after her. He caught up with Jackie walking rapidly toward a store down the street. They were being followed and they could both sense it. Ty thought that the second entity had begun its attack on her, and it wanted revenge on both Ty and Jackie. She kept right on walking and Ty had to tell her to slow down before she tripped. The wind blew hard and it kept Jackie jumping at everything that moved. She appeared totally shaken.

It was obvious from Jackie's face that she was feeling the pressure of something powerful and frightening. The entity tried to dominate Jackie's mind. Ty felt badly for her, but there was nothing he could do. He had gambled by leaving Caroline back at the apartment with Ben. His heart was pounding just as hard as hers was now, and he was also frightened. Ty was almost certain that Caroline was all right, and he was hoping he had made a sufficiently strong impact on the situation already that no evil spirit would try to challenge him over his daughter. Joseph had committed the sin of despair, and Ty's Confidante had said, "Things have been done. It's time for you to move on."

Ty understood that the Confidante's people had defeated Joseph. But it was not over and they did have to leave.

Jackie went into Safeway and purchased a pack of cigarettes. She came right out still walking quickly and managed to light a cigarette while moving nervously from side to side all the way back to the apartment.

Ty hustled up the stairs to the apartment and opened the door. Caroline and Ben were sitting watching TV. Everything was fine; there were no signs of any spirits inside the house at that moment.

When Jackie reached the top of the stairs, she sat down in a chair on the balcony for a long while. Ty left her alone, and went inside to spend time with Ben and Caroline. A few minutes later, he went upstairs where they still had plenty to smoke and waited for Jackie, who had remained outside smoking a cigarette. He tried not to think about what she was going to go through. He just did not want anything happening to Caroline.

Jackie finally came inside but spent a long time fumbling around in the bathroom. Ty went down to check on her after a while, and asked, "What are you looking for Jackie? Can I come in?"

Jackie opened the door and seemed to have calmed a bit. Fortunately, she decided to slow down on her crack consumption.

"The night is young," she acknowledged.

"Whatever works for you, works for me," Ty replied.

"I'll be up in a minute," she said.

Caroline had begun dozing off, so Ty laid her down and said goodnight to Ben as he went on back upstairs. He knew Jackie would be up all night behind the power of the drug and the spirits who remained outside the walls in a supernatural state of anarchy. She wasn't going to sleep tonight because of fear, crack and an inability to understand what was happening to her.

She paced up and down the stairs all through the night and went into and out of the bathroom and the one bedroom.

Ty fell asleep and woke up the next day and found out that Jackie had gone to work. She had also called and talked to Caroline. Caroline told Ty that Jackie had to work that night as well.

"Two shifts?" Ty was upset. He picked up the phone and called Jackie.

Jackie chilled him out, assuring him, "I'm all right and we need the money."

She did come to the apartment first before going in to work the night shift at the restaurant. Ty and Caroline drove Jackie to the restaurant so Ty could take Caroline to McDonald's for dinner. They never did get Jackie's car registered and back on the road, but it had quit running in any case.

The sun was down by the time they got back to the apartment with McDonald's for themselves and Ben. Caroline and Ty ate in the kitchen while Ben ate in the room, and played video games.

Ty finished eating and went upstairs. There was a lot of dope left from the night before. He took a couple of puffs and then the phone rang. It was Jackie. Ty became shook up all of a sudden.

"Is everything okay?" he asked.

"Yes, but I am ready to leave work," she told him.

"Be right there," he responded.

"Why is mommy coming home so early?" Caroline wanted to know.

"Mom is probably tired, Caroline." Ty explained.

He started out the door with Caroline right on his heels. He looked outside and saw the strangest things happening, and called to Ben who immediately came to the door where they both looked out, eyes popping.

Ty focused his eyes on the park across the way and started to make out what looked like an army of dead things, from lurching, wretched animals to disfigured humanoid shapes moving through the evening fog, disappearing and reappearing as they shambled through the foliage.

Ben said that he could see these things too and was not staying at the apartment alone. He got his shoes and left with Ty and Caroline.

They left in a hurry, Ty wondering what would have happened if he had left Ben behind. There was a bad smell in the air.

Ty pulled up in front of the restaurant and Jackie came out and got into the car acting very bubbly and surprised to see Ben. Then, out of nowhere, Jackie turned to Ty, her eyes straight as a razor, and asked him: "What are we waiting for? Thirty days for what? Let's leave as soon as possible."

She finished speaking and fell silent. Ty could almost sense that army of the dead they had seen in the park closing in on them from all directions. Gone is where he truly wanted to be as well.

Jackie and Ty kissed and Caroline cheered, while Ben said, "Cool! Let's go!" They drove away toward the apartment actually singing. All Ty needed to do now was order the truck, which he did the next day.

Their last night at the apartment was the 14th day of July. Ty had Jackie and Caroline spend the night with Oma, a lady he had known all his life. This lady treated him like a son always, even through his worst times. Ben and Ty stayed at the apartment and finished loading the truck, then packed up the Honda onto the trailer by two o'clock the morning of July 15. They had the apartment cleaned and ready for whoever wanted it. Ty locked the apartment door and put the key in the drop box at the office.

Ty and Ben drove away from the apartment complex like thieves in the night to Oma's house. It was too late to knock on the door, so they tried to make themselves comfortable in the car outside her house. Ty didn't care as long as Caroline and Jackie were safe and warm inside. As Ty and Ben sat staring out at the night, the sky began to darken.

All of a sudden a guy who lived in the area all his life, an ex-pro football player who Ty knew of, came walking up to the car out of the dark. It startled Ben who initially thought it was one of the walking dead. But Ty just rolled down the window and started talking to him. Ty couldn't understand too much of what the one time football player had to say because he was so high. Ty did notice though that the roof top of Oma's house was lined with a mysterious shadow. Ty didn't care to focus on the rooftop just yet. He was trying to keep up with what was happening with this haggler standing by. The run down, skeletal-looking man stared over at the big truck next to Ty and Ben.

"Is that your truck?" he asked.

Ty just nodded.

"I heard you might be leaving."

Ben was very quiet and Ty could see he was uncomfortable and staring at the house that Jackie and Caroline were staying in.

"Not might! I *am* out of here in the morning!" Ty expressed himself firmly, but the shabby-looking man—not that Ty looked any better—just stood outside the car and didn't say anything for a long while. And it was cold that night. The atmosphere began to tighten with an intense chill. The wind picked up to the point where the car shook, and it didn't seem normal. Ty began to expect the unexpected.

Ben continued staring at Oma's house, and it was still a mystery to Ty because he couldn't tell what Ben was looking at.

"Hey man, you need to get on down the road," Ty demanded of the visitor.

All of a sudden the man reached through the window of the car with a speed that was deceptive for a man so drunk, stoned, and worn out looking, and snatched the only blanket Ty had and ran away with it. Ben refocused his attention and he and Ty watched the man run down the road alongside that mysterious dark shadow that lifted from the roof of the house.

Ty started his car and drove to the location where the hardcore street people stayed and found the thief. Ty got their blanket back and then Ty and Ben spent their last night in Seaside on the worst street in town.

Ben was in a bit of shock seeing the many different propositions being carried out in cars, on the sides of houses, and on that street between men and women.

The sale of dope of all kinds was being conducted from several houses. There were so many people of all ages going in and out of these places, the faces of so many prominent people mixing freely amongst the living dead.

Ty sat in his car and watched the evil huddled in every corner, dark holes, and cracks on that street. The smell was so bad you would have thought the sewage drains had run over. Temptation in the grandest manner was right under Ty's nose.

Ty was recognized by many who came to his car window but he refused their dope. He had money in his pocket. But it would remain there. There were so many lost and unwanted souls residing in this area. Ty was amazed at how he was able to channel into this world of darkness without being frightened by the sounds that he heard and seeing the communication between the dead and around the living, all happening on the sidewalks of this nasty street. The evil force had moved into this town and controlled this city, one of many in the world, and when the patrol cars rolled through, they kept right on going.

Ben had dozed in and out of sleep, and Ty continued to wipe the hidden tears back while he endured Satan's massacre of minds and souls, thinking about how this could be the rest of his life.

As the sun began to rise, the living dead returned to their holes and cracks, like vampires getting back into their coffins, leaving the last of the stragglers rambling through the debris along the curbs of the street.

When the sun overwhelmed the darkness Ty understood clearly that his residence in the city of Seaside had come to a close.

He started his car, having gotten a good look at the drug-decimated street and at the corrupted creatures that walked its paths.

He then drove Ben back to meet Jackie and Caroline. As Ben got out of the car, Ty told him to let Jackie know that he would be right back.

Ty then headed to Steve and Rene's house to pick up Cass. Rene had already left, but Steve came out of the house. Steve and Ty both had tears in their eyes because it had been a while since they had last seen each other and it hurt. Ty had now lost fifty pounds and weighed 132 pounds of nothing. He didn't have much money, but he was alive and his bags were packed and ready to go.

Steve fed him and then gave Ty some items to take with him on the trip. He wished his brother-in-law well. Ty stood firm for all he could, like a man making a last stand. Steve gave Ty and Cass one last hug. Ty was dead-tired and had a long trip ahead of him. He had to go, and waved good-bye.

Cass and Ty drove back to Oma's house to meet up with Jackie, Caroline and Ben. Oma had made Ty clean up. She washed the clothes he had on and made food for them to take on the trip. It would save them money that they didn't have.

That $5,000 that he was supposed to have when they left town ended up at $450.00. It took awhile, but eventually everything was ready. Thanks, kisses, and hugs were exchanged with Oma and then Jackie, the kids and Tyrone left.

Ty and Jackie decided to make one last stop at the hair shop to get their hair done and to surprise whoever was there. Hair shops were good for spreading gossip around, so everyone in town would soon know that they had left town. Ty sensed shock and dismay from the owners of the shop.

"I told you all I was leaving one day and today is that day," he said.

They knew that this was the last stop and said their last good-byes and waved as Ty drove that big Ryder truck, leaving town pulling Jackie's car behind him.

Ty hit the highway, Jackie following close behind in his car with Ben and Caroline in the back seat. Never did he look back. Ty looked straight at the sun and followed it toward the metropolis that everyone called "Sin City." But to Ty, Jackie and the kids, it was a new beginning.

As they drove out of town, Ty prayed:

"All I can say is that I must live through this experience twice because I must write this story down for everyone to read. I don't want to ever go through something like this again. Lord, please find this to be positive; a way to help better and strengthen the future. Let it shine light on the life of everyone who reads it. And may You be with us always. Dear Lord, the faith we have in You will remain in us forever, continue to love and watch over and have mercy on our souls.

"I thank my mom Gail Burns, for giving me life, teaching, and sharing her love with me, and I thank the Lord more so, for He is merciful, and I am blessed and most grateful.

"Amen."

Age alone won't save Mon

REVERSING A DECISION by Monterey's Historic Preservation Committee, the City Council decided that this old house, at 881 Newton Street in New Monterey, isn't worth preserving.

Orville Myers/
The Herald

>>KNIGHT RIDDER>

Afterword

The House at 881 Newton Street is-or was, at least-very real, as are the events depicted in this book. The names were changed for personal reasons.

The only name that wasn't changed was that of Joseph Hillzer, the eight year old who killed himself following a tragic accident involving a dynamite cap left near the Newton Street home by a careless grading crew.

*

Shortly after the characters in "The Beast Beneath" departed Seaside, California for Las Vegas, the house became the subject of some controversy as it was scheduled to be demolished. But the house's age-it was known to be at least 50 years old-drew the attention of Monterey's Historic Preservation Commission, which denied the owner permission to sell.

Oddly enough, however, residents of the area were not anxious to preserve the structure, no matter its antiquity. The Monterey City Council unanimously reversed the commission's decision and, according to a local newspaper article written by reporter Calvin Demmon, "Even Neal Hotelling, a local historian who has often been sharply critical of city decisions about historic properties, said he could see no point in preserving the Newton Street residence."

Ansel Thoeni, president of the New Monterey Neighborhood Association-a hard line group that normally fights to preserve old buildings-seemed equally sanguine on the subject and offered no objections to the house's destruction, which was completed shortly thereafter.

The Epilogue

Jason and his girlfriend spilt up, but have a daughter together. They live near each other in the Bay Area of California.

Carla and John also have a daughter. They married and divorced. Carla is now remarried to a wonderful man with two boys and a daughter of his own, and they are now expecting their first child together. They also live in the Bay Area.

John lives in the Bay Area as well and stays in touch with his daughter.

James died. His brother Jack took over the construction company and is doing very well. Their friend Joe still works with Jack, and they live in their California hometown.

Matt and Tim, the power lifters, are both doing well and have families. Matt lives in Las Vegas, and Tim resides in California.

Nancy lives in the Bay Area of California, and she and Jackie are still best of friends.

Steve and Rene spilt up and went their separate ways. They didn't have any kids together. Steve went on to become a millionaire in his business, and he and Ty remained very close.

Frank and Lucy and the girls still live in Arizona and are doing fine.

Eric and Stacy have two girls but their dog, the brother of Cass, died. They are doing very well living in Carmel Valley, California.

Kevin lives in the Bay Area of California with his family and has left his number at the barber shop for Ty to call him. Ty has yet to attempt to get in touch.

Pat and her husband are still going to church faithfully with their family and are both retired. Officer Martin has been battling heart problems; it runs in his family. His wife, Ty's niece, has two children that are healthy and happy, and they are all handling the situation.

Aaron continued to live the same lifestyle and has been in and out of prison.

Donna followed Ty and Jackie two months later to Las Vegas with her son. The pair drove an old vehicle and made it all the way to the bus station Downtown before it broke down. There she traded it for a new bicycle. She found Jackie and Ty, and when she was ready to move in to her first apartment, Ty helped her with the move. Donna is now a supervisor in a very good job. She bought herself a home where her son lives with her, and is now working on a second home. She stays in close contact with Jackie and looks fantastic and is a wonderful friend.

Kenneth and Kelly moved from their apartment and bought a house in their hometown in California. Later, they came to visit Ty in Las Vegas and then went back to their hometown and sold their house all in a weekend. They now live in Las Vegas, where they have a beautiful home. They are doing more than well. Ty and Kenneth are together all the time. Ty and Kelly have put the past behind them and they get along when they see each other.

Larry lives in the Bay Area with his third wife-to-be. She has two boys of her own. Larry is now in contact with all of his kids regularly. He also attended Carla's wedding and the reception which was held at Jackie's and Ty's home. The whole family has reunited. Ty, Jackie, and Larry spent a memorable afternoon and evening together with uncles and aunts and guests, after many years apart. The Lord blessed us all with that day.

Ben turned out to be one heck of a young man. He graduated with his class, he got his diploma and learned a wonderful trade. His lives with his wife to be, and Ty, Larry, and Jackie are very proud of him. He and his fiancée are expecting their first child any day. They also live in Las Vegas.

Ty has not been in contact with his Confidante, but he knows where she is.

Ty, Jackie, Caroline, and Cass are one happy family. Jackie has three more years on her job, before she retires. She is an office administrator. Caroline turned out to be a beautiful young lady, and is working toward an acting and singing career. Ty is back to his old faithful skills, sharing his fitness plans with people in need of better health. Cass is old now, but you could never tell she was 90-

plus in dog years, as Ty's got her eating well and exercising also, when she is not hanging out around the pool.

In the six years since Ty left his hometown the loss of lives, and livelihoods were inexcusable, as it was overtaken by the drug, crack cocaine.

Ninety percent of Ty's male class of '76 is either on the streets, hooked on drugs, in prison, or in their grave.

"I want to thank you from my heart for all your support!!"

"God All mighty!" for he is my Lord and Savior.

The Healer & Priest (East Coast)

Jade Wyckoff (Daughter)

Judith Wyckoff (Step Mom)

Rosemary Rogers (Best Seller Author)

Bill Kunkel (Editing Co.)

Gustavo Santana (Artist)

Marco Coronado (Agent)

Myron & Velda Wyckoff (Dad & Wife)

Lulu.com